BOONE

Frederic W. Burr

Other books by the author

Mutinies
(Race and the Navy in the 1970's)

The Ring

The Return

Lens Capture
(The Camera Sees the Truth.
All of It)

For the Love a Pete

Grab an Egg
(And Shave It)

Uphill

Old Salts, New Navy

The Persian Paradox

Letters from Peru

An Uncertain Sea

Abby's Maze

Abby's Test

Journeys

Unaccountable

This is a work of fiction. Names, characters, places, and incidents are products of the authors' imagination, or are used fictitiously and are not to be construed as real. Any resemblance to actual events, locales, organizations, or persons, living or dead, is entirely coincidental.

Copyright ©2021 by Frederic W. Burr -- All Rights Reserved.

Except for appropriate use in critical reviews or works of scholarship, the reproduction or use of this work in any form or by any electronic, mechanical, or other means now known or hereafter invented, including photocopying and recording, and in any information storage and retrieval system, including electronic transmission, is forbidden without the written permission of the author. For permissions: fwburr@gmail.com.

Table of Contents

ONE *1*

TWO *11*

THREE *23*

FOUR *34*

FIVE *43*

SIX *58*

SEVEN *69*

EIGHT *75*

NINE *86*

TEN *102*

ELEVEN *113*

TWELVE *125*

THIRTEEN *134*

FOURTEEN *143*

FIFTEEN *153*

SIXTEEN *159*

SEVENTEEN *170*

EIGHTEEN *184*

NINETEEN *196*

TWENTY *202*

TWENTY-ONE *211*

TWENTY-TWO *218*

EPILOGUE	*223*
AUTHOR'S NOTE	*224*

Everything in the world is about sex except sex. Sex is about power.

Oscar Wilde

ONE

IT WAS LATE SPRING. Boone was sitting behind his desk, having a cup of coffee. He had completed his report on a runaway teen girl he had tracked down for her worried parents and was trying to concentrate on a front-page story in the Monday morning edition of the Albany Times-Union. It had something to do with a Troy police detective embezzling union funds. But the soft breezes coming in through the open window, and the noises from Swan Street traffic below kept distracting him. He could also hear the muffled sound of Marianne talking on the phone, even though the door between their offices was closed.

He thought about asking the corporate landlord for a solid door between the two spaces. After all, if he could hear her, she, and anyone else on her side, could hear his discussions with clients. The landlord might kick, after already having subdivided the empty office next to his so Boone could bring on Marianne as his office manager. But he wasn't worried about that. The onsite manager for the building, Carl Murphy, who went by Murf, owed Boone to the tune of tens of thousands of dollars in alimony payments.

Two months earlier, Murf had come to him seeking advice. He suspected his ex-wife had a live-in lover, but he couldn't prove it. If he could, under the terms of his divorce agreement, he could discontinue paying her alimony, which amounted to a third of his take-home pay. It took Boone ten days to come back with a series of photographs and bills from the ex-wife's trash proving ongoing residence of her boyfriend. Instead of billing the manager, Boone agreed to take it out 'in trade' to Murf's relief.

Two sharp knocks on the interconnecting door interrupted his reading. Marianne opened the door and stood inside the doorway. He gave up on the paper and laid it on his desk. Looking at her, he said, "Yes?"

Although she looked better to him than he had ever seen her, he kept such thoughts to himself. Six months earlier, she was as gaunt as a concentration camp survivor. She had just escaped from kidnappers working on behalf of the FBI, but only after her captors had tortured her and beaten her to within an inch of her life. After her release from the hospital, the forces behind her kidnapping renewed their efforts to locate her.

Boone became her protector (his ex-wife always accused him of having a white knight complex). To neutralize the threats against her, they had to bring on an armed private security team. Afterwards, it took months of therapy for her to recover from the ordeal.

"Mr. Boone, that lawyer, Clive Townsend, just called," she announced. "He's on his way over, and he'll be here any minute. I get he helped both of us with the FBI, but why does he have to act like you're . . ." she hesitated and smiled before finishing, "his personal dick?"

Stifling a laugh at her use of the slang term for detective, Boone shook his head before responding. "He's like that," he said. "But let me remind you, he sends us a good deal of work, and always pays our bill, and promptly."

"I know," she said, "but . . ."

Townsend's throwing open the hall door as he burst into Boone's side of the office interrupted the conversation. She looked at the lawyer, then at Boone, and retreated to her desk, closing the door behind her.

As always, Townsend's attire was immaculate. He was wearing a lightweight gray pinstripe, and a well-pressed lilac blue dress shirt with a navy and red silk rep tie. But with his buzz-cut hair, a nose that had been broken more than once, cauliflower ears and hands like a dockworker, no one would mistake him for the shy, retiring type.

Boone leaned back in his chair and put his boots up on the corner of the desk. "You wanted something?"

"Yeah," Townsend replied. "I got this client, . ."

"And it would appear, so do I," Boone said, pointing at Townsend.

Townsend grimaced, shook his head, and said, "Hold it, will you?"

"Holding."

"My client is probably going to be accused of murdering her boyfriend late last night."

Boone remembered a breaking news story on the morning news, something about a developer's son dying, and a suspect in custody, but nothing else.

"Her current boyfriend?" he asked.

"No. Well, I don't know. Could be her ex-boyfriend. I'll have to check on that."

Boone snorted. "If he's dead, regardless of who killed him, it's probably safe to say he's her ex-boyfriend. So how did he die?"

"She allegedly jammed a letter opener into his left femoral artery."

"Ouch! That'll leave a mark. How'd he let her get that close to him? I mean with a letter opener?"

"The ME says there's lipstick on his baby maker."

"So, he was naked?"

"Naked enough."

"Somehow, I'm getting the impression he wasn't her ex-boyfriend. No charge for that clue. Let's cut to the chase. What do you want me to do?"

"I want you to do what you do best," Townsend said. "Investigate. You know, nose around, run it down."

"You don't need to get so technical," Boone said. "Do the police like her for it?"

"Oh yes. And the news media, fucking jackals they are, they do as well. Seems the recently deceased was the eighteen-year-old son of Abe Creekson."

"Creekson, the developer?"

"Calling him a developer is like saying Moses was just dropping off a memo. And it's not just that. He's a donor to the state GOP."

"Really? I thought Republicans were an endangered species in Albany."

"Most New York Republicans are just moderate Democrats in disguise. But Creekson has always been a contrary sort."

"What about your client?"

"She comes from a middle-class family. Both her parents work, and they live in the Legends subdivision. In Bethlehem."

Boone knew that area well. Less expensive homes on the outskirts of the more well-off areas around New Scotland Avenue.

"Where is she now?" he asked.

"They're putting her on a psych hold at Albany Medical Center. When they tried to question her last night, she was incoherent."

"So, she hasn't been arrested, or Mirandized."

"Correct."

"But you're not convinced that she's guilty?"

Townsend sighed. "My client is a friend of my younger daughter."

"Samantha?"

"Yes. Sam. She swears Gerry would never do such a thing."

"And Sam is an excellent judge of character, is she?"

"She's beyond her years at fourteen. I've met Geraldine, and I have to say she doesn't seem the type."

"How old is your client? I mean, if she was engaged in, . . . you know. Fourteen seems young for that, doesn't it?"

"Geraldine is sixteen."

"Sixteen? That still seems pretty young to me."

Townsend again shook his head. "You need to get with the times, Carl. So, you willing to get into this? You don't seem all that busy."

Boone took his boots off of the corner of his desk and sat up. "Sure. What are friends for? Send me over what you have, and I'll get right on it."

Townsend reached into his inner suit-coat pocket and extracted several folded sheets of paper. Laying them on Boone's desk, he said, "Here you go. That's enough to get you started. Crime scene photos, along with a check for your usual retainer, will be here some time after lunch."

It always impressed Boone how quickly Townsend could get crime scene photos, which any other defense counsel would not see until well along in discovery. He suspected the man had some serious juice with the forensic techs in the Albany PD.

Townsend stood up. "And you should try to dress better," he said. "Might make your clients take you more seriously."

Boone looked down at his navy T-shirt from Katz's Deli in New York City, with '*Send a salami to your boy in the Army*' emblazoned across the front in bright yellow script. "What's wrong with this?"

Townsend made a dismissive gesture with one hand as he left, without closing the door behind him.

As Boone looked over Townsend's sheets. Marianne worked on the end of the month financials for the office. And fumed. As much as she enjoyed working with Boone, she was unhappy with being a mere employee, working on financial statements, scheduling appointments, and answering the phone. She had an MBA from Northeastern, for Pete's sake!

Marianne didn't need the job from a financial perspective. She wanted work that challenged her. And she wanted to own something, not just work at it. She wanted to be a partner and thought 'Boone and Bell' had a nice ring to it.

But, as always, that train of thought led her to feel guilty, as though she was ungrateful. When she was at her absolute weakest, Boone was there to protect her while she recovered from her injuries and guard her family as well.

When he offered her the job, her parents were overjoyed. Their daughter would have gainful employment with a trustworthy employer who would keep her safe. More than once, her father told her to be grateful for the life she had. And she was.

But she still wanted more.

* * *

That afternoon, a courier dropped off a large manila envelope from the law firm of Cooper/Townsend addressed to '*Carl Boone, Albany's Finest Shamus.*' Boone chuckled at Townsend's offbeat sense of humor.

Inside, under a check payable to Carl M. Boone, LLC for one thousand dollars, were a dozen crime scene photographs of the late David Creekson. Like always, the pictures themselves were brutal in their brightly lit, tack-sharp details, sparing nothing and no one.

Geraldine appeared to be sitting on the side of a bed, wearing only panties. Looking closely at the shots of her face, loosely framed by her disheveled blonde hair, Boone could almost count the individual grains of eyeliner streaking down her cheeks. Her eyes were widened in shock. The pupils themselves were mere pinpoints centered in hazel irises. Her mouth was open as if she were about to say something. The fingertips of one hand rested on the point of her delicate chin. For someone supposedly in the immediate proximity of a sliced femoral artery, there was barely a trace of blood spatter on her breasts, and none on her hands or arms.

In contrast, David Creekson's body, lying in an unmade bed, wearing only a T-shirt, looked like a study of a young man's body by Michelangelo. His thighs and calves appeared well muscled, with little to no fat. His flaccid penis was tucked almost modestly around the scrotal sac. But for the handle of a letter opener sticking out of the inside of the young man's left thigh, and the large stain of dark red blood seeping into the bedclothes under his legs, he could have been modeling for an advanced course in life drawing. The absence of any defensive wounds puzzled Boone. But even more baffling was the boy's apparent state of relaxation while being stabbed deeply in his leg.

From Townsend's materials, he knew the murder took place in the Creekson home. From what he could see in the photographs, it was probably in the victim's bedroom. Boone would love an opportunity to look around the room where the crime took place. But since he was working for the accused's defense attorney, that would prove difficult to impossible. Regardless, he didn't think Geraldine Bronson was good for the murder. None of this seemed to hang together.

He picked up Townsend's materials, leaving the photographs on his desk, and walked into Marianne's side of the office. Handing her the sheets, he said, "See what you can find out about these people, can you?"

She brightened as she reached for the pages. "Thank you! These month-end financials are boring the hell out of me."

TWO

THAT EVENING BOONE SAT down in the living room after his microwaved dinner to look over the case. After placing Townsend's printout, the crime scene photographs, and the results of Marianne's online searches in separate stacks on his coffee table, he went through each one, reading and analyzing carefully. The goal was to develop an overview of the case. He thought better when he started fresh.

Marianne's results helped him make sense of the photographs. David Creekson was no stranger to illicit drugs, according to his supposedly sealed juvenile records. Depending on what he was on, he may not have even realized someone had stabbed him in the leg. And Geraldine's pinpoint pupils, and incoherence during questioning, suggested she might have taken some type of opioid. David's post-mortem and Geraldine's lab work should provide some answers.

David was a junior in Christian Brothers Academy, a top-ranked private school. It did not surprise Boone to see he was active in the school's cross-country and swimming teams. However, he was not a standout student, barely maintaining a B average with no AP courses. He did not appear to have a presence on social media. David's family lived in the Buckingham

Lake-Crestwood area, in a home with an assessed value of $675,000. Abe Creekson, David's father, was a commercial developer with the Albany Corporate Park, among other large projects, to his credit. Marilyn Creekson, David's mother, served on the boards of several local area charities.

Geraldine Bronson was a sophomore at Bethlehem Central High, a well-regarded public school. She had no juvenile record or disciplinary notes in her file. Unlike David, she was holding an A-minus average while carrying two AP courses. Aside from the usual tagged photos and comments on her friends' posts, her Facebook and Instagram social media accounts were unremarkable. Her family lived in the Legends of Bethlehem neighborhood in a home assessed at $330,000. Stanley Russell, her stepfather, was an actuary for Aetna. Her mother, Elaine Russell, was a physician's assistant whose first husband, Captain Roy Bronson, died in Afghanistan in a 'blue on green' attack.

Boone made a note to touch base with Itzy the next morning. Itzy was one of his confidential informants from his career with the New York State Police. If anyone could provide him with a lead into dealers supplying high-school students, Itzy could, given his never-ending interest in controlled substances. Boone would also try to speak with David's mother at some point.

He also listed Samantha Townsend as a contact, at least to develop a list of Geraldine's friends as a starting point in his investigation. He couldn't think of anyone else to add to his list. That would come later. Hopefully, he would discover how, when, and where the two met to allow him to develop an understanding of their relationship. The more questions he asked, the more questions and people to ask would come to mind.

After putting everything back into his accordion file, he put one of his favorite Art Pepper albums on the turntable. As the music played, he poured himself the last of the Jameson's eighteen-year-old Irish whiskey Marianne had given him last Christmas. Then, he sat down in his one extravagant piece of furniture, the Eames lounge chair. With his ankles crossed on the ottoman, he listened to the music, sipped the whiskey, and felt a nearly overwhelming sense of pity for David, and for Geraldine.

* * *

In the psych ward at Albany Medical Center, a crash team was trying frantically to save Geraldine Bronson's life. Although her incoherence and pinpoint pupils upon admission indicated an opioid overdose, before they could administer naloxone, she went into respiratory arrest. After suctioning her mouth and oropharynx and intubating, they placed Geraldine on a mechanical ventilator.

The naloxone only made matters worse. Less than one-tenth of one percent of patients experience cardiac arrest with naloxone. Geraldine was that one patient out of a thousand to suffer such a side effect. She was pronounced dead at 10:37 that evening.

Among other early findings in her postmortem was the discovery of trace amounts of fentanyl in her blood, so even without her reaction to naloxone, she was doomed before arriving at the hospital.

* * *

Tuesday morning, Marianne announced Townsend was on the phone for Boone.

"Did he say what he wanted?"

"No, just that it's important. He sounded upset."

Knowing there was very little that could penetrate Townsend's emotional armor, Boone was curious. He reached for his handset to take the call.

"Boone here."

Townsend got right to the point. "Geraldine died last night. Looks like whatever she took was laced with fentanyl."

"Damn! So now what? Want me to close my file?" Boone knew the Albany PD would shut down their investigation and close the file after the death of their principal, and only, suspect.

"No! Not on your life. My daughter is, . . . I've never seen her so distressed. She, . . . Damn it! *We* want answers!"

Boone could hear his caller taking a couple of deep breaths. Eventually, with no prompting, Townsend admitted, "And besides, I promised Samantha."

"Understand. Listen, when might I be able to speak with Samantha?"

"Why?"

"Just to get a list of Geraldine's friends, and for anything about Geraldine she wishes to share with me, that's all."

"Sounds reasonable. Shouldn't be a problem," Townsend said. "I'll get back to you."

After hanging up, Boone reflected on the fact that he'd never heard Townsend sound so emotional. Having a client emotionally invested in a case was a double-edged sword. On the one hand, they paid their bills, but that was only so long as they saw results. He would not want to disappoint Townsend, and not just because he was a client.

Looking up at his wall clock, he realized it was time to leave for his meeting with Itzy. Marianne was on her line. He sent her a text to let her know he would be out of the office until after lunch. She responded with a thumbs-up tap back.

As he walked the few blocks down to the Albany Distilling Company bar for his meeting, he thought about the brevity of Marianne's response to his text. She had been reticent all morning. Was she upset about something? Angry with him? Going over their recent interactions, he could not think of anything he might have done that would upset her. Zipping up his jacket against the stiff breeze coming off of the Hudson, he concluded Marianne was simply busy, and didn't have time to type out a reply text.

He was glad to get inside the bar and out of the wind. Springtime weather in Albany was always an uncertain proposition. Balmy one day, ball freezing the next. Looking around, he spotted Itzy at the far end of the bar, sipping on what looked like a triple. Boone unzipped his jacket as he walked the length of the bar, taking a seat next to his informant.

Itzy was wearing his trademark mismatched sneakers, tattered jeans, and a thin windbreaker over a sweatshirt. His sharp features and greasy reddish-brown hair suggested someone down on his luck and barely getting by. Boone knew differently but played along.

"What are you drinking? Ironweed?" Boone asked, referring to the barrel-aged bourbon made by the distillery with New York State grain.

"Hey, it's cold outside, and I told the bartender this is on your tab," Itzy replied, his eyes darting nervously around the room as though expecting imminent danger from an uncertain direction.

Boone made a small laugh - *humph*. "You haven't changed, have you?"

"I say stick with whatever's working." Then, turning to address the bartender, he pointed at his drink and said, "Barkeep, another one of these, yeah?"

"Triple Ironweed on the rocks, right?"

"Yep."

Then, looking at Boone, Itzy said, "And what'll you be having?"

"Coke," Boone said, not at all surprised by Itzy's resourcefulness. "I have to work this afternoon."

"Coming right up." The bartender poured the second triple and placed it in front of Itzy with a flourish. He then filled a glass with ice and used the hand-held dispenser to top it off with Coke.

Sitting the Coke in front of Boone with a thin-lipped smile, he said, "Here ya go. Anything else?"

Boone shook his head and looked around the bar. It was not quite 11:30. The place hadn't started filling up with the lunch crowd.

"So, what do you need, captain?" Itzy asked.

"Drugs. Not for me, but who are the main suppliers in the area high schools?"

"You gotta be kiddin' me. There's dozens of 'em. Any particular school?"

"Yes," Boone said before taking a sip of his drink. "CBA and Bethlehem Central."

Itzy sighed. "The guy, at least the main guy at CBA, doesn't like me handin' his name out. But I can have him call you. Okay if I give him your, . . . you know, your private number?"

Boone carried a pay-as-you-go burner in addition to his iPhone. He used the burner strictly for contacts with his network of informants.

"Sure. What about Bethlehem Central?"

"I'm not sure on that one. Gimme some time?"

"Okay."

"Is this on the, you know, the usual arrangement?"

"You're drinking it," Boone replied. "Get me a name for Bethlehem, and we might do this again."

Itzy looked like he wanted to protest but seemed to think better of it. Boone stood up, laid a twenty on the bar and said, "Keep the change," to the bartender.

He made his way out of the bar. If he stayed for lunch, Boone knew Itzy would order the most expensive thing on the menu. For lunch, he ducked into the Hollow Bar and Grill on North Pearl for a Reuben.

* * *

Back in the office, there was a message on his desk to call Townsend. Townsend told him Samantha would speak with as many of Geraldine's friends as she could about meeting with Boone after her friend's funeral, set for Friday.

Boone also learned from Townsend that David Creekson was on the date-rape drug GHB when he was murdered. Known colloquially as 'blue nitro,' 'cherry meth' and 'great hormones at bedtime', Boone knew GHB was a depressant inducing a state of euphoria and relaxation. Boone felt this might account for David appearing to be asleep when someone pushed a blade deep into this thigh.

Finally, Townsend told him forensics had determined there were no fingerprints on the letter opener. From the photographs and this additional evidence, to suggest that Geraldine played any part in the murder was implausible. Not that it would have made any difference by then, as far as she was concerned.

He made notes of this additional information at the bottom of Townsend's materials.

* * *

Two days later, Boone had a call on his burner cell identified only as 'Unknown Caller.' He answered, "Yeah."

"You a cop?"

"No. How'd you get this number?"

"From Itzy. You want to know about CBA?"

"Just one buyer in particular."

"Sorry. I don't reveal the names of my buyers. They like their privacy, you know?"

"This one's dead, so I don't think he cares."

"Huh. What's the name?"

"Creekson."

"You're talking about David, right?"

"Who else?"

The caller was silent for such a long time, Boone asked, "You still there?"

"Yeah, I'm here. David bought a lot of Gina from me, usually one point fivers."

"What's that? A one point fiver?"

"One and a half grams. It's all he ever wanted."

"And when you say 'Gina,' you mean GHB?"

The caller laughed. "Yeah. Georgia Home Boy, whatever you want to call it. But David used it almost exclusively."

"He ever tell you why?"

"Not in so many words. But he said it was for himself, not for a girl."

"Was that important? I mean to you."

"I prefer to sell to people for their own use, not to use on someone else. Ya know? Blowback is a bitch, and I don't have time for it. That's what I told him."

"And all of your buyers tell you the honest-to-God truth, do they?"

"Hey! It's better than nothing."

"What did he say, about why he wanted the drug for himself?"

"Hard to say. I mean I tried understanding him, but . . . It was like he wanted to have sex but wanted to be on the nod at the same time. Not be there for it, you know? I didn't twig to it exactly."

"Anything else you can tell me?"

"Nope."

"Thanks. You gotta name?"

"Yeah, but not for you. Don't bother writing down this number. The next thing you hear will be this phone hitting the trash. Tell Itzy we're square."

Boone added notes to Townsend's printed material summarizing his conversation with the dealer.

THREE

It was overcast and cold on the morning of Geraldine Bronson's funeral. Boone found it hard to believe that last Monday he was wearing a T-shirt to work and had his office windows open. At least the lining was still zipped inside his trench coat. He could not remember the last time he had taken it out. Another example of the benefits of procrastination.

After reaching the Albany Graceland Cemetery on Delaware Avenue, he found the internment site easily enough. After parking, he walked carefully over the soggy ground to stand on the fringe of the gathered crowd. Geraldine's friends were clustered together, talking among themselves. All of them he could see wore short black skirts, dark jackets, and black tights. The other mourners stood disbursed around the gravesite while the priest spoke in subdued tones.

As the cloud cover increased, he felt sharp, icy droplets on one side of his face. Looking up, he could tell snow was on the way. Being early May, it wouldn't amount to much, but it was still annoying as hell.

Fortunately, to signal the conclusion of the funeral service, the priest was splashing what Boone took to be holy water from a small hand-held stainless steel sprinkler. Mourners began drifting away from the gravesite as the casket was lowered into the ground. A couple he took to be Geraldine's parents were in the middle of the group leaving the gravesite. The man was struggling, doing his best to help the woman at his side remain on her feet, even as she appeared to be bent over with grief.

Seeking shelter from the mixed precipitation, Boone moved to stand under a tree. A younger girl detached herself from the group of Geraldine's friends. Boone recognized her immediately as Townsend's daughter, Samantha. She was the only one of the younger people sensibly dressed, wearing slacks and a longer coat. He waved his hand on his outstretched arm to attract her attention, and she hurried towards him. He looked around as she approached but didn't see her father.

When she reached him, he extended his hand, saying, "I'm very sorry for your loss."

"Thank you," she replied, barely touching his hand with her gloved hand. "I just want to tell you that three of Geraldine's friends will talk to you now, and that two others want to sit in before they decide. Is that okay?"

He smiled and nodded. "That's more than okay, Samantha. Thanks. I was thinking we get inside somewhere. How about Nicole's Restaurant just up Delaware Avenue? I checked, and they're just now open, so we can get a table away from the lunch crowd."

"Sure," she said. "I'll ride with them, and we'll meet you there."

"You'll all fit in one car?"

"We came in a SUV with third-row seating. It's fine."

"Great then. See you."

He watched her hurry back to the group. As they talked amongst themselves, he walked to his car, feeling the cold air now stealing down his neck towards his chest and back. At least the heater worked in his twenty-six-year-old Crown Vic.

The car came cheap at a police auction. The rusted exterior showed three different colors in its panels and trunk. Inside, the upholstery appeared to be ripped out and badly stained, with no sign of a radio or CD player. Overall, the car looked like crap on four wheels, but the engine, transmission, differential, and heavy-duty shocks were in top shape, and his run-flat tires looked barely broken in. He sometimes thought the car could be dropped grill first from a crane onto concrete and still run.

Arriving at the restaurant ahead of the girls, he went inside and requested a table for eight off to one side of the dining area. As two wait staff moved around square tables to accommodate his request, he put his iPhone on silent mode, and brought up his VoiceMemos app.

With the phone inside his shirt pocket, he could record the conversations for later review. With New York being a one-party consent state for recording conversations, he knew he was on solid legal footing. He also suspected these girls, being fourteen to sixteen years of age, might be hesitant to speak freely if they knew he was recording the conversation, although he suspected at least one of them might do the very same thing.

After taking a seat, to keep up appearances he pulled a small notepad out of his inside jacket pocket and a ballpoint pen to make the occasional note. At that point, the six young ladies bustled in through the restaurant's entrance. Standing up to help them locate the table, he waved at Samantha. She waved back and led her five friends over.

With less chatter than he expected, they all sat down. A waitress approached them, and Boone asked, "Does anybody want anything? Coffee? Danish? Soda? A sandwich? It's on me." The girls began talking amongst themselves as the waitress handed out menus. During the ongoing babble, he ordered coffee and a cheese danish for himself.

The waitress got orders from Samantha and two of her friends for tea and donuts. After she left, Boone spoke to the group.

"Thank you all for coming. My name is Boone, Carl Boone. I am a private investigator, and . . . "

Samantha interrupted him. "They already know what you're investigating. I told them you're working for my dad, looking into Geraldine's, . . . uh, . . . well, her death."

"Thank you, Samantha," he said, taking a moment to make eye contact with each of the girls. "First, I'd like to extend my condolences to all of you over the loss of your friend. And thank you for taking the time to speak with me today. Before I ask any questions, do any of you have questions for me?"

"I do," the girl closest to him said. "My name is Judy. You're not a police officer, are you?"

"No. I'm a private investigator. That means I try to help my clients discover, or investigate, things that are important to them by developing evidence through leads, public records, and cooperating witnesses or people close to whatever I'm looking into. People much like yourselves.

"Sometimes attorneys need help to find a witness, or surveillance. Insurance companies will sometimes want to hire someone like me to watch someone claiming to be disabled, or injured, who they suspect of lying. I have no authority to arrest anyone, and I am bound by the same laws that bind everyone else. For what it's worth, I am a retired detective from the New York State Police Bureau of Criminal Investigations."

"Do you have a gun?" another girl asked.

"And your name is?" he asked.

"Sorry. I'm Karen. I was in Geraldine's homeroom at school."

"Well, Karen, yes. I have a gun. In fact, I have several firearms."

"I'm Mary," another girl interjected. "Gerry and I were besties. Do you have a gun with you?"

Boone chuckled. "No, I'm not carrying today. I didn't think I would be in any danger with you young ladies." As they chuckled, he thought about his 1911 Colt .45 caliber semi-auto locked in the glove box of his car, along with the detachable holster from his shoulder rig.

The two girls, who were curious, but as yet unwilling to speak with Boone, maintained their silence. He was more interested in what they might have to share than the three willing to be interviewed.

"Anything else?" he asked.

The six girls sat silent as the waitress began placing the orders in front of Samantha, Judy, and Karen. Before leaving, she refilled his coffee cup.

"Tell you what I'd like to do," he said. "I will ask a general question, and I'd like anyone who has anything to share to put their hand up. Some of the information you want to share with me is private, and I understand. I'll give each of you my card before we leave so you can touch base with me later if you would rather speak in private. Okay?"

Samantha and her three friends nodded. To Boone, they appeared to be interested if not excited, despite their streaked eye makeup. He wondered if it was due to being questioned by a private eye, just like on television.

"First, did any of you know, or know anything about, Geraldine's boyfriend, David Creekson?"

Both Judy and Karen put their hands up, and Boone nodded at Judy to speak first.

"He wasn't her boyfriend," Judy said, nodding for emphasis. "He went out with, . . ." she hesitated, her eyes flitting towards one of the two girls who were only sitting in on the conversation, "with other girls. But I think Gerry wanted to be his girlfriend."

Karen leaned over to speak to Judy. "He was asking what we know about David, not Gerry."

"Sorry," Judy said. "I guess I misunderstood. I didn't know that much about David, myself. Just more about Gerry."

"Karen, is it?" Boone asked.

Karen nodded. "I didn't know David personally. I mean, he went to CBA and all. But everyone who knew about him knew his family was rich. He could have any girl he wanted."

Turning back to Judy, Boone asked, "How do you know Geraldine, Gerry, wanted to be David's girlfriend?"

"She told me so," Judy replied. "She said she would do whatever she had to."

"That's not true," Mary interjected. "You make her sound like some kind of slut!"

Samantha held her hand up and asked, "Can I say something here?"

Turning to her, Boone said, "Go ahead, Samantha."

"Thank you," she said. "Gerry and I were in the same AP class, Human Behavior. We talked a lot before class, and after since it was before lunch. I don't think she would have done anything, like Judy says, to be David's girlfriend, but she had definitely set her cap for him, you know what I mean?"

"I do," Boone said. "Thanks. Can anyone tell me if Gerry had boyfriends before meeting David? Did she go out with anyone regularly?"

Mary spoke. "Not really. I mean, she went out on dates and such, but no one all the time. As far as I know, anyway."

The other two girls looked at each other and shrugged.

"This is a delicate question," Boone said, "but I hope you understand I'm asking only to have a better understanding of the facts. If you prefer to contact me later to talk about this, that's fine. Was Geraldine sexually active?"

Judy and Karen both blushed. Mary, who Boone thought of as Geraldine's closest friend in her age group, shook her head vigorously.

"I don't think so," Mary said. "I mean, she would have told me if she was."

Samantha added, "I kinda doubt it. We only had the one AP class together, but we had lunch together three days a week, and I never got that impression. There are rumors about what she did that night with David, but I don't see how anyone knows for sure."

"One last thing, at least for now," Boone said. "Did Geraldine ever experiment with drugs?"

The three girls spoke nearly in unison. "No!" "Absolutely not." "Her parents would have grounded her into next year if she ever did."

He looked at Samantha. "What do you think? Did she?"

Fixing Boone with a level gaze, she answered, "I would be very surprised if she did. I know she didn't even like taking anything stronger than aspirin if she had a headache."

Boone took the time to make a lengthy note after Samantha's remark. Upon finishing, he looked up and said, "Thank you all. This has been very helpful. I'd like to give each of you one of my cards in case anything else comes to mind that you think might be relevant."

He reached into his pocket for a handful of cards and stood up to hand them out. Each of the girls took a card before getting ready to leave. One of the two observers held back as everyone else headed for the front door.

"My name is Kelly, Kelly Richardson," she said as she took Boone's card. "There's something about David I think you should know. I'll call later today."

"Thanks, Kelly," he said. "I look forward to it."

After she left, he returned to his seat. He put his notepad and pen back in his pocket, then ended the VoiceMemos app on his iPhone. Looking at the time recorded on the file, it appeared to match up with the time spent speaking with the girls.

He planned to add notes about the funeral, and the girls' remarks, on the Townsend printout when he returned to the office. The morning was productive, in his opinion. Aside from looking into Gerry's drug habit, if any, and talking with her parents, there wasn't much left to investigate on that side of the file. David Creekson's funeral was the next day, and he would be there.

FOUR

THE DAY AFTER GERALDINE'S funeral dawned clear, but brisk, with smaller altocumulus clouds sailing through a sharp blue sky. Parked in the Lady of Angels Cemetery in Colonie, Boone sat in his car waiting for the Creekson funeral party to arrive. He sipped coffee from his thermos and reflected on the two obituaries. Geraldine's was heartfelt, her family's pain over her death resonating with each line. In contrast, David's read like a résumé, or an essay written to satisfy a college admission requirement.

From what little he knew of the two families, he was developing a sense that the Russell home was a loving family-centered home, while the Creekson's were all about business. And the business of doing business.

As he finished his third cup of coffee, he saw three police motorcycles with flashing red and blue lights in a wedge formation clearing a rise in the cemetery roadway ahead. They were followed by the hearse and a long black limo. A lengthy procession of high-end sedans and large SUVs trailed behind the limo. An Albany PD cruiser, its light bar and grill-mounted lights flashing red and blue, brought up the rear. If he didn't know better, Boone would have thought some important politician was the subject of the procession.

As mourners exited their cars and began walking towards a large seating area under a white overhead canopy, six young men wearing dark blue military uniforms gathered at the rear of the hearse. Boone took them to be classmates of David Creekson from the Christian Brothers Academy.

After most of the attendees were seated, the funeral director opened the rear of the hearse and slid the casket on its collapsible trolley out of the vehicle and onto the pavement. The casket itself was draped in a Christian Brothers Academy flag. The six pallbearers took up their positions on either side of the casket and lifted it off of the trolley.

Boone waited until all the stragglers had taken their seats before getting out of his car. He took his time following the pallbearers as they struggled up the hill to the gravesite. He wondered how much money old man Creekson donated to the Academy to merit this sendoff for his son.

Standing behind the seating area, Boone watched the priest go through the ceremony. He thought the entire production was over the top, considering the deceased was a mediocre student with a drug habit. After the priest finished, the six pallbearers took the Academy flag off of the casket and folded it up and tucked it under one arm. Unlike an American flag, there was no presentation to the parents.

Maybe the academy needed it for future funerals?

Boone stood off to one side as those in attendance filed out of the seating area, heading for their cars. Abe Creekson was wearing dark glasses, and the woman on his arm, presumably David's mother, wore a black veil over her face, making their expressions unreadable. They walked past Boone, erect and with no visible sign of emotion, returning to the limo parked behind the hearse. Neither of them so much as glanced in his direction.

Driving back to his office, he thought about the best way to approach the Creekson's and drew a blank. Maybe Marianne would have an idea. If, that is, she was speaking to him. For the past week, she had been curt, clearly unhappy about something. For the life of him, he had no idea what was troubling her.

* * *

Back at the office, he could tell Marianne had been in while he was at the funeral. His coffee cup, which he normally left unrinsed on his desk, had been washed, dried, and put up on the top of the file cabinet. It was upside down on a napkin, next to the Mr. Coffee coffeemaker. The carafe, discolored from old dregs burned into the bottom of the pot, had been scrubbed to like new condition. Looking around, Boone could tell she had even dusted.

Imagining Marianne muttering to herself as she cleaned up the office, he felt himself duly reproached over his slovenly habits. And for her to feel relegated to such a lowly function. He knew that never having asked her to pick up after him, much less clean the office, would not be a defense. Maybe bringing on a cleaning service would make amends?

There were no messages on his desk, and nothing that required his immediate attention. After making notes about the Creekson funeral, he went to the gym.

He liked going to Best Fit on Central Avenue. It was on the way to his apartment, and it had an excellent selection of equipment and weights. And unlike other gyms he'd been to, nearly everyone who went there was serious about their workouts. They didn't stand around and talk with whoever might be around, or stare at their phone, before leaving after a minute or two on a machine they never bothered to wipe down.

After thirty minutes on the treadmill, fifty pushups, ten two-minute planks, and some work with the free weights, he did another fifteen minutes on the treadmill to cool down. After grabbing his streetwear from his locker, he walked quickly to his car for the drive back to Latham. The Best Fit neighborhood after dark was not one of Albany's safest. He usually showered at home.

***

Later that evening, Boone was sitting down to one of two or three meals he could cook quickly from scratch—spaghetti with store-bought sauce, frozen meatballs, and a sausage link. He liked to cook, but not if he was eating alone, which seemed to be the case almost exclusively. He had a small bag salad for a side, and a glass of Chianti. The liquor store clerk claimed it was an excellent 'value' wine, whatever that meant. Knowing nothing about wine, Boone went with the recommendation, figuring if he was out six bucks, it was no loss.

He was halfway through dinner when his iPhone signaled an incoming call. He dabbed at his mouth with the folded section of paper towel he used as a napkin before answering.

"Boone here."

"Is this the detective?" It sounded like a young girl. The voice was familiar, but he couldn't place it.

"Yes."

"This is Kelly Richardson. Remember me?"

"Refresh my recollection. The name rings a bell."

"I was with Gerry's friends yesterday after the funeral? I said there was something about David you should know?" Like most young girls, she ended each sentence with a rising inflection, as if asking a question.

"I remember you. Don't you want to come to my office to talk about this?"

"No. My parents are out tonight, and it's my only chance to talk with you. You know, in private?"

"Okay. Let me get paper and pen." He laid the phone down and walked over to his small living room for his notepad and ballpoint pen.

Back in the kitchen, he picked up the phone, and said, "I'm back."

The line was silent for a time until she said, "I'm not sure this is such a good idea. It's embarrassing, you know?"

"Look. I know your name, but that's it. If you don't want me looking for you to follow up, it's better to just get it off your chest now."

"Okay," she said.

He waited until she was ready to talk, having learned anyone about to reveal something embarrassing needed a moment or two.

"I dated David," she finally said, before adding quickly, "but it was only one time!"

"Uh huh."

Another lengthy pause. He watched his spaghetti sauce congeal.

"I knew his family was rich, and he was, you know, cute?"

Under the girl's name, he wrote 'D.C.', 'one date,' 'rich' and 'cute.'

"I don't want you to think I'm a put out, but him being, . . . well, you know, . . . we went to his house? His parents were away at something or other. I figured he might be thinking about sex, and I was willing to at least, . . . oh. This is so embarrassing."

"This won't go any further," he said.

"You swear?"

"I do. Promise."

"Okay. Anyway, we went upstairs to his room. We sat on his bed, and started necking, and pretty soon, we were, you know, taking our clothes off? And like all of a sudden, he stopped. He said he wanted to take this pill, that it helped him relax and enjoy it better or something like that? He asked me if I wanted anything, and I said no. Drugs scare me."

Boone waited for what seemed to take five minutes. "Is that it?"

"No. This is the odd part. He said once he was totally relaxed, I could do whatever I wanted, once I, . . . you know, got him hard?"

He wrote 'necking,' 'drugs,' and 'stimulation.'

"Did he say what it was he was taking?"

"'G' I think he said. Or something like that. I didn't know what that is. But I told him I didn't want to take anything."

"And then what?" he asked.

"What do you mean?"

"Did he actually take the pill? I don't want to pry," he said. "You can tell me as much or as little as you want."

"That's pretty much all I have to say," she said. "He took the pill, then laid back on the bed. After he was like passed out, I just got my clothes on and left. I mean, that's just so weird. He might as well just be a, . . . you know?"

Boone suspected she didn't want to admit she knew what a dildo was, or how it was used, and let it pass. He wrote down 'dressed,' and 'left.'

"Just one question,' he said. Before she could say anything, he asked, "How did you get home?"

"Oh. I called my dad to come and get me?" she replied, sounding relieved. "He asked me how my date was, and I just said it was okay."

"Did David ever call you again?"

"No. And that's fine with me."

"Anything else?" he asked.

"No," she said. "I have to go now." She ended the call.

He looked at his phone and made a note of her number and fleshed out his notes.

After covering his dinner to reheat in the microwave, he sipped the wine and went over his conversation with Kelly. What she told him seemed to fit with what he learned from David's dealer. He wanted some sort of sexual experience, but with only minimal personal involvement. From all the evidence, and the remarks by her friends, he was even more convinced Geraldine was the innocent player in whatever went down at the Creekson residence. He would need to speak with the boy's parents. That would not be easy.

FIVE

Monday morning, Boone drove to work from his apartment, resolved to speak with Marianne. He wanted to get her thoughts on the Creekson matter, but also to clear the air. If there were any shortcomings on his part to cause her discontent, he wanted to know.

Unfortunately, with two rear-end collisions on the infamous Latham traffic circle, US Route 9 became a parking lot for a good thirty minutes. By the time he reached downtown Albany, he was fuming. After parking, he was twenty minutes late and three blocks away from his office on Swan Street. He started off at a brisk pace, still fuming. But his mood was tempered by the time he reached the building, thanks to the mild spring air.

Going through the door on his side of the office, the first thing he noticed was the smell of freshly brewed coffee. And it was not that burnt Starbucks crap he picked up at the store. The door to Marianne's side of the office was open, and he could see her on her line. It sounded like she was booking an initial appointment for a new client. The day showed promise.

She looked over at him, smiled and gave him a thumbs-up gesture, and he knew that somehow, all was right with the world. He fixed himself a cup of coffee, raised the blackout shades behind his desk, and cracked the windows for some fresh air. By the time he sat down behind his desk, she was walking into his office with an appointment slip.

He looked up at her. She said, "Boss, we have to talk."

"Oh," he said, realizing all may *not* be right with the world after all. He proceeded with caution. "About?"

"What I'm doing here."

"Fair enough. What's on your mind?"

"First, here is an appointment slip for you. New client, tomorrow afternoon at two. A woman, but she wouldn't say what she needs. May I sit down?"

He extended his hand out, palm up in invitation. She sat down, resting her clasped hands in her lap.

Before she could speak, he said, "I noticed you cleaned the place up over the weekend. That's not what I expect you to be doing, and I'm going to bring on a cleaning service. I should have done it before, I know . . . "

"I don't mind the occasional pickup," she said. "But . . . "

"But?" He raised his eyebrows.

"You know I have money. I don't need this job for income."

He nodded. "I understand."

"I want to have more responsibility. You get to go into the field, go to funerals, talk to people, question witnesses and meet clients. I don't want to be just a secretary." She leaned forward with an earnest expression on her face. "Do you know what I mean?"

"Ah . . . um, . . . yeah. I think I do. But . . . "

"Here it comes," she interrupted, frowning. "Don't 'but' me. I will be forever grateful for what you did for me, and my family, and I love working with you. I just want more, and I don't want to feel like I need to be protected all the time."

"So, what do you want from me?"

"Not sure, exactly. I was hoping you'd have some ideas. I mean, it is your office."

He leaned back in his chair, one finger to his cheek with his chin propped on the remaining clenched fingers, staring at her with half-lidded eyes.

"Tell you what," he finally said.

She leaned against the back of her chair and said, "Tell me!"

"I'll try to involve you more in the investigation side of things, including going into the field, . . . "

As she said, "Really? Like, . . ." he held up one hand to forestall her, adding, "In *some* cases. You can keep your own records of your time, and the work you're doing. And don't forget to include your computer searches. And we'll see how things go. Okay?"

"That sounds good," she said. "But why do I need to keep records?"

"So we can bill the client, at a reduced rate for your time, of course. But, if you decide you want to go further and one day apply for your own license, you'll need some serious, detailed documentation. It's not enough to be employed by a licensed investigator."

"What's involved in applying for a license?"

"I think you need three years of what the licensing bureau calls," here he made air quotes, "full time investigating experience. But you'll need to check that. Maybe see if you can find some online records where people have had hearings on their applications."

"Wow! Three years? Full time? That's going to take a long time," she said. "Okay. I'll start keeping records."

"Fine." He looked at his coffee, which by now had gone cold. Standing, he picked up his cup and said, "Let me take this down the hall to heat it up."

"I can do that for you," she said.

"No," he smiled. "That doesn't count as investigative work. I want you to dig up everything you can on the Creekson parents, and we can talk about that file when you've finished. I want to pick your brain. Okay?"

She stood up, announcing, "I'm on it, Boss!"

* * *

When he got up to go to lunch, she was still at her desk, pecking at her keyboard while staring at her monitor. Occasionally, she would make a brief note on a legal pad.

"Can I bring you something back?" he asked.

"No," she said. "I brought something in from home, and I'll just take lunch down the hall. But I have to tell you, the Creekson's are very interesting people."

On returning from lunch, Boone found a two-page printout on his desk, and the door between the two sections of the office was closed. He picked up the printout and read what it had to say.

Abraham (Abe) Isaac Creekson: b. March 15, 1957. Grad. Maimonides Hebrew Day School 1975 w/3.8 GPA, SUNY Albany BS in Business Econ, 3.2 GPA 1979; m. Marilyn (Bennet) Creekson 2002, one child (David). No indication of children by other women.

Chairman, CEO of Creekson Developers, Inc. (CDI), comp. $3.76 M/annum plus % of net rents from major projects, incl Albany Corporate Park.

Misc. income from subsidiaries of CDI. Mbr Temple Israel of Albany, non-observant but deducts $175K/yr on 1040 Sched A. Mbr Albany Country Club (Tennis—Family), primarily business-related. Joint chkg Citizens Bank Westmere branch on Western Ave w/wife Marilyn. Avg daily bal $15—20K. Corporate banking account Schwartz Heslin Group, Inc. Small private acct HSBC avg daily bal $4–5K from which he w/draws $400—500 cash weekly.

On USPS informed delivery for home mail, mostly junk mail, some personal correspondence. Corporate mail not on informed delivery. Also a PO Box on New Karner Road Post Office, but according to his credit profile, no bills go to that address. The box is not on informed delivery.

Black AmEx VISA acct, credit limit $75K, aside from Albany Country Club and other routine charges, most interesting—runs tab at Waterworks Pub every 10 days to 2 weeks ranging from $300--$750. Residence: 246 Rafts Way on Buckingham Lake Park–PVA $675,000 (6br, 7baths, 5-car garage). Drives 2-yr old Mercedes-Maybach S Class in his name only, NY tag DVLPR. Clean DLA. Donates under his name to GOP, but also to Democrat PACs in undisclosed larger amounts (2 and 3X).

He shook his head in amazement at the information Marianne could pull off the internet. She once told him, "If it's anywhere on the internet, I can find it." *So much for personal privacy*, he thought.

The existence of a secret post office box, as well as a private account for cash transactions, suggested a dimension to the father one would not expect, especially considering he regularly frequented one of Albany's well know gay bars. He knew there could be perfectly reasonable explanations for everything Marianne had so far uncovered, but how to flush them out would be the challenge. He flipped to the next page to read about Marilyn Creekson.

Marilyn (Bennet) Creekson: b. June 18, 1975. Grad. Bethlehem Central High School 1993 w/4.10 GPA, Sr. Class Pres. And Val, SUNY Albany BA in Medieval & Renaissance Studies, 3.8 GPA 1997, m. Abraham Isaac Creekson 2002, one child, David. Subj and child received DNA testing through ancestry.com confirming maternal relationship. No evidence of any DNA test for Abraham, the father of record.

Employed as curator Albany Institute of History & Art (AIHA) 1998 until marriage to Creekson in 2002. Serves on boards of AIHA, Alliance for Positive Health, Grassland Bird Trust, and MD Assoc. Active in Albany Country Club Tennis tourneys. No mail accounts aside from home, small private checking acct Citizens Bank Westmere branch, avg daily balance < $1,000, infrequent cash w/drawals. Carries Black AmEx VISA (infrequent use) and Citizens Bank VISA account, credit limit $20K, no unusual activity. 2021 Toyota Avalon Hybrid. Deducts < $25k/yr to Albany area charities on 1040 Sched. A (mostly subj's board seats). Clean

DLA, no political donations, registered Dem. No religious pref.

After reading through Marianne's search results a second time, Boone felt he was developing a sense of the Creekson family. The father was a man who spared himself nothing, even to the point of carving out a private dimension to his life.

The mother was the nurturing, selfless force in the family, more concerned to the point of caring deeply for people and causes less fortunate than herself (even if she seemed dry-eyed and stoic at her son's funeral). Talking with the father would be a waste of time. It was Marilyn Creekson he wanted to interview. He asked Marianne to step into his office.

Resting his hand on her reports, he said, "This is great work. Great work, really. I'd like you to look over the rest of the file, starting with Townsend's information, my notes, and the crime scene photos. Then, tell me what you think." He slid the file across the desk towards her.

"Can I take this home?" she asked.

"Copies, yes. Also, it's probably time we scan everything into a digital file. We'll talk tomorrow."

"Got it." She stood, picked up the file, and began walking to her side of the office.

Hesitating at the door between their offices, she turned to face him, and added, "And thanks."

"For what?"

"For listening to me."

* * *

The next morning, the two of them sat down on either side of Boone's desk to go over the file. Marianne sat in one of his mis-matched client chairs, holding her copy of the file in her lap.

"Did you have time to go over everything?" he asked.

"Yes, I did. It's an interesting case."

"What's your first takeaway from everything so far?"

She pursed her lips in thought before answering.

"Geraldine's as much a victim as David." Marianne held up one finger. "She didn't kill anyone, but . . ." then holding up a second finger said, "whoever did him didn't want her to be around to talk about what happened."

"And what do you base those conclusions on?"

"She had no significant blood spatter despite her proximity to the injury. There were no fingerprints on the weapon, even though she didn't appear to be wearing gloves. She had no known history of drug abuse, according to her friends. Did you ever hear from anyone dealing at her school?"

"Not yet. I'll have to talk to Itzy, . . . "

"Who?"

"Itzy. He's CI Seven in my notes. You'll get to meet him someday, and I won't be doing you any favors when you do. Anyway, I'll call him. From what her friends say, I suspect there won't be anything new there."

"Anyway," she continued, "As I was about to say, someone gave her an opioid mixed with fentanyl. It doesn't take much fentanyl to kill someone. I think it was deliberate, but I have no idea how she got it, or who gave it to her."

"Any idea who the 'someone is?"

"Not exactly," she replied. "But it has to be somebody close, since it took place in the boy's bedroom. Maybe one of the boy's parents, but I don't see any motive."

"Yet," he said.

"Yet," she agreed.

"Okay. We're on the same track. Can you find out anything about the mother's schedule? I don't think I'm going to get much out of the father, but the mother may be helpful. I don't think I can call her up and ask for an appointment. I'm going to have to catch her unawares."

"Will do."

BOONE WAS just finishing his chicken parmesan sub at Miranda's Deli on Columbia Street when he received a text from Marianne.

Yr 2:00 is here EARLY.

Shit! he thought. *It's not even one o'clock!* After paying his bill, he hurried back to the office. The plan was to be back in time to check for food stuck in his teeth and gargle with mouthwash. Once inside the building, he ducked into the men's room to rinse his mouth out several times. Checking his breath, he realized it was hopeless. At least he had the foresight to wear a sports jacket and tie that day.

Entering through Marianne's door, he said, "Any messages for me?" hoping to sound to the client business-like and efficient, if not professional.

Marianne followed suit. "No, Mr. Boone. Your two o'clock is waiting in your office." She held up a notepad with 'Judith Hirschhorn' written in large block letters.

"Thank you, Ms. Bell," he said. He stepped into his side of the office. A well-dressed woman looking to be in her early to mid-thirties, was sitting on the sofa. She looked at him and said, "Mr. Boone?"

Her long blonde hair was artfully streaked and expertly arranged around delicate features.

She looked to be of eastern European ancestry. From her pantsuit, blouse, and jewelry, it was obvious she came from money, serious money. As he looked at her, he was rapidly lowering his guess as to her age.

"That's me," he replied. "And you must be Ms. Hirschhorn."

She tried to smile even as the skin around her eyes and the cords in her neck tightened "Yes. I'm sorry for being so early, but . . . I'm frightened. I don't know what to do." Her lips pinched into a grimace as she reached into her purse for a handkerchief.

Dabbing at her eyes, she then looked up at the ceiling, trying to forestall tears. He carefully shut the door between the two offices, walked behind his desk and, gesturing at one of his client chairs, said, "Why don't you have a seat, and we can talk?"

She composed herself and began to rise from the sofa. As she stood, Boone found himself struck dumb by her incredible beauty. He was relieved to be able to recover his power of speech by the time she had taken a seat in front of his desk.

"What can I do for you, Ms. Hirschhorn?" he asked.

"Judith, please," she said.

"And Carl is fine with me," he replied. "What seems to be the problem you need help with?"

She glanced at the door separating the two rooms of the office to make certain it was closed before saying, "I'm being extorted."

He made a note on his legal pad, and looking at her, said, "Have you notified the police? Or the FBI?"

"Oh no," she answered. "I can't do that."

"Why not?"

She took a deep breath. "Because it could expose me to criminal prosecution. And," she added, "don't write that down. This is all confidential, right?"

"Well, Judith, up to a point, it is," he answered. "If you tell me you're about to commit a crime, or have killed someone, for example, I can't not notify law enforcement. But otherwise, . . . "

She made a fleeting smile. "No, I haven't killed anyone. At least not yet."

"Why don't you tell me about the extortion. Who is it, what do they want from you, and when do they want it? And I'll need some idea of what it is they have, or know, that might cause trouble for you."

Again, she glanced nervously at the door separating his office from Marianne's area. "I'm not certain, but I believe it's a business partner of my husband's."

"What makes you say that?"

"This person, he seems to know things about me that my husband does not know. At least that's what I think."

"You said 'he.' Do you recognize his voice?"

"No. I can tell it's a man calling me, but he muffles his voice."

"Can you tell what number he's calling from?"

"No. My phone just shows 'Unknown Caller.'"

"What does he want?"

"I don't know."

"Can you at least give me a hint about these *things* he knows that your husband doesn't know?"

With eyelids lowered, as if she could not face Boone, she said, "Certain photographs of me in, ..." she glanced off to one side as she continued, "shall we say, compromising situations?"

"Oh. What do you want me to do?"

"I don't know."

Boone suspected she knew what she wanted him to do. She just couldn't bring herself to tell him.

SIX

"SO, LET ME GET THIS straight," he said. "You don't know what this person wants, you can't go to the police because you're afraid of being prosecuted. You suspect your husband's business partner may be behind this, but you're not sure what you want me to do. Is that right?"

"Yes," she replied, smiling tightly.

"Sounds like my kind of case," he said. "Not only do I get to run around looking for clues, but I also get to figure everything else out from the get-go."

"I can pay you," she said.

"You can't pay me enough," he replied. "My detective's manual says I need to know at least two of the following four things to get into a case."

He held up his hand, extending his index finger. "The who." He added his middle finger. "The what." Holding up his third finger, he added, "The why." And finally raising his little finger, he said, "The want. What the client wants."

"You actually have a manual?" she asked.

"Well, no. That would probably be helpful as well. Look. I have other things to work on.

When you can decide what it is you're looking for, call me and we can try this again. Okay?"

With her eyes downcast, she sat in the chair for a moment before sighing and looking up at him.

"I'm sorry to waste your time," she said.

"It's okay. Here," he said, holding out one of his business cards. "Call me if you think I can help you."

She took his card and slipped it into a side pocket of her purse. She stood and said, "I really am sorry."

He stood up to go around his desk and open the door for her, but she reached for the doorknob before him and let herself out. He stepped into the hall and watched her spectacularly successful backside as she walked down the hall to the elevator.

Given his track record, married, divorced, with an estranged nineteen-year-old son, he had accepted his status as a lifelong bachelor. But Judith Hirschhorn was so blindingly magnificent, he would have considered marrying her just to sit and look at her all day long.

Back inside his office, Marianne was standing by the side of his desk, smirking. "Was she as gorgeous leaving as she looked arriving?"

"I wouldn't know," he said. "I was checking the weather."

She laughed. "Here." She handed him a piece of paper. "Marilyn Creekson's schedule at the Albany Institute."

"She posts her calendar on the internet?" he asked in disbelief.

"No. But the Albany Institute's calendar is there for anyone to see. Well, anyone on the dark web, that is."

"Huh." He glanced at the paper and saw that Marilyn Creekson would be at the Institute's reception desk that afternoon until closing at six o'clock.

"Look," he said to Marianne, "I'm going to the Institute for a couple of hours. While I'm gone, see what you can find out about Judith Hirschhorn."

"I'm on it, Boss!"

* * *

It was a ten-minute walk from his office to the Albany Institute, and still a pleasant day. As he paced, Boone thought about Judith Hirschhorn. She told him she was worried about some compromising photographs that her husband did not know about. He wondered if that was true. But claiming to have no idea what the extortionist wanted simply made no sense at all.

If he were the client, his first want would be to recover the photographs along with any negatives or copies. But in the digital age that was simply unrealistic. The extortionist would have to be neutralized, convinced somehow that further pursuit of his target would entail more risk than any benefit he could hope for. Given that the client seemed to be well off, the nature of the photographs was probably the key to the whole thing. The more compromising they were, the harder it would be to turn off the extortionist.

If he wound up taking Judith's case, he'd need to know a lot more about the husband and his business partner. As he approached the front steps of the Institute's entrance, he checked the time. It was coming up on three. He wouldn't need three hours to interview Marilyn Creekson. But he suspected he would be lucky to get ten minutes from her.

Stepping inside, he took off his sunglasses and looked around. The foyer was well lit from windows above a curved staircase. Two marble statutes of partially dressed women wearing fabrics artfully draped below their waist stood off to one side of the staircase.

"May I help you?"

He turned to his left and recognized Marilyn Creekson. She was sitting behind a curved counter. A name plate in front read simply 'Reception.'

She was wearing a light gray cinch-sleeved blazer with a lace trimmed ecru blouse. From the information Marianne had provided, he knew she was in her mid-forties, but she looked much older.

Walking slowly over to her, he said, "Ms. Creekson?"

"Yes?"

"Ms. Creekson, my name is Carl . . . "

She interrupted him. "You were at my son's funeral. I remember your standing behind the tent. What were you doing there?" As she spoke, she put her hands on the counter and stood up.

"Ms. Creekson, my name is Carl Boone, and I am a licensed private investigator. I don't mean to cause you any distress. Friends of the young woman who was with your son on the night he died have asked me to look into their deaths." He knew he was hired to investigate only Geraldine's death but hoped that mentioning David as part of his investigation might help.

Her eyes widened in shock; her mouth hung open for a second. After running one hand through her hair, her eyes tightened to slits. "You mean you're working for that slut who killed my son? And you want to talk *to me?* Are you serious?"

Boone saw that any chance for a productive discussion was rapidly slipping away. He went for broke.

"Ms. Creekson, Geraldine Bronson's friends all assure me she was not a slut. Whoever killed your son also murdered her. Did you know that?"

"She's dead?" Marilyn's mouth turned down into an ugly frown before she spat out, "Then good! I hope she rots in Hell!"

"I'm sorry you feel that way, . . ." he said before being interrupted again.

"I don't care what you feel, or think," she screamed, her voice shaking. "But I never want to hear from you or see you *again*! Will you *please* leave?"

He placed one of his business cards on the counter and said, "I understand. I only want to find out who was behind the murders of your son and my client's friend. If you change your mind, . . . "

She picked up his card, tore it in half and flung it to the floor in front of her counter. In a lowered voice, she said, "If you do not leave this instant, I am calling security."

He held up both hands, palms towards her and fingers slightly spread in a gesture of surrender. "I'm leaving," he said. "If you change your mind, please call me."

Turning around, he walked back to the main entrance and left the building. Taking his time to return to his office, he was thinking the day was not working out so well after all. In terms of clients, he was zero for two. At least he had patched things up with Marianne for the time being.

As he walked, Boone's burner cell phone signaled an incoming call. Flipping it open, he saw it was from CI Seven.

Hmm. Itzy calling. Maybe with a name for the Bethlehem Central dealer? He pressed the 'talk' button.

"Boone here."

"Hey man, what did you say to Jitter?" Boone recognized Itzy's voice.

"Jitter? Who the hell is Jitter?"

"You know. The dealer at CBA. You talked to him, right?"

"I talked to somebody who said he knew something about drugs at CBA, and that he sold to David Creekson. He said to tell you that you and him are square. I was waiting for you to call me about Bethlehem, . . ."

"Fuck Bethlehem," Itzy said. "Jitter's dead!"

"What?"

"Yeah! They found his body behind the Karner Road post office. What else did you say to Jitter?"

Karner Road post office. Rings a bell somehow, Boone thought. "Nothing," he said. "I listened to what he had to say, and that was it. Maybe I asked him a few questions. Do they know how he died?"

"One tap back of the head. Execution style. They figure he's been dead at least a week."

Boone thought it had been longer than a week since he spoke with Jitter. There was probably no connection between Jitter's murder and their conversation. *But why does the Karner Road post office ring a bell?*

Itzy interrupted Boone's thoughts. "You still want that Bethlehem dealer? I might have a name for you."

"Forget it. He won't be able to help me. I doubt this person was a user."

"It ain't a 'he.' They's girls that deal now. But whatever. You need something, let me know." Itzy broke the connection.

Boon closed the flip phone and continued his walk, thinking about the New Karner Road post office.

It was half past three when he walked into his side of the office. Marianne was at her desk, and not on her line.

"Anything happen while I was out?"

"Nope. Quiet. But you'll never believe what I found out about Judith Hirschhorn."

"Probably not," he said as he poured himself a cup of coffee. Turning to face the doorway between her workstation and his office, he said, "So tell me."

Marianne turned her computer display to face him. He was shocked to see a much younger Judith Hirschhorn on the screen, naked and posed in such a way as to leave nothing to the imagination. Despite himself, Boone blushed.

"Meet Joy September," Marianne said. "I feel like I need a shower after looking at this stuff."

He turned his face away and closed his eyes, as if to give the on-screen Judith privacy.

"I don't need to see that," he said.

"It's okay," she said. "You can look now."

He opened his eyes and turned his head slowly to face Marianne. "What else do you know?"

"Plenty," she said. "I found her on Wikipedia right away, but after doing some serious searching, I found her juvenile record, mostly shoplifting and such. I also found her arrests for solicitation and promoting prostitution, along with some minor cocaine busts. She was born Lula Mae McCracken in Little Rock, Arkansas, and got into porn at the age of 17. In her twenties, she became Joy September. Now in her early forties, she's found respectability as Mrs. Judith Hirschhorn."

"Did you find out anything about her husband?" he asked, beginning to feel disappointed if not profoundly depressed over his earlier attraction to her.

"Oh yes," Marianne said, sounding much chirpier than he felt she had a right to.

"Entriken, that's a Scottish name I gather, meaning 'son of Andrew,' from the Greek Andreas. In his mid-sixties, he is the senior member of Hirschhorn Enterprises, a limited liability partnership originally located in Poughkeepsie, NY, now in Cohoes, NY. At the beginning, Hirschhorn was a publisher of skin magazines and novelties, like playing cards featuring nude women."

"As Entriken became less involved in the business, Hirschhorn Enterprises became a second-tier adult entertainment business. Their website doesn't tell you much, but I've been able to determine the company, through a network of shell corporations, owns adult book stores, a video production company that makes adult films, and it appears to run a stable of so-called female escorts in the upstate area. Why do they call these businesses 'adult,' anyway?"

"Good question," he said. "Maybe we should think about background checks on potential clients before the first interview, what do you think?"

"I agree," she replied. "What do you want me to do if she calls back?"

"See what she has to say, I guess," he said. "A client is a client. If we only took cases from good, upstanding citizens, we'd have no business at all."

He decided to hit the gym on the way home.

SEVEN

Thursday morning, Boone saw a short article in the Albany Times-Union headlined 'Body discovered behind New Karner Road Post Office.' Below the headline was a pixilated copy of a high school yearbook photo of a young man from two years back.

With long, dark hair combed low over his forehead, the boy wore an expression of scorn. His smile was asymmetric with one corner of his mouth turned slightly up, the opposite corner pulled downward, insincere. The eyebrow over the upturned corner of the lip was raised, exposing more of the white of the eye. The overall effect was a sneer, not an expression of reassurance or trustworthiness.

Under the photo, the article read:

> ALBANY—Authorities on Tuesday afternoon were investigating the partially decomposed remains of a young man found in a grassy area behind the U.S. Post Office on New Karner Road in the city.
>
> Dental records were used to identify the body as that of Jerome Bruno, a 2019 graduate of Albany Central High School. Known to his classmates as Jitter, Bruno lived with friends in the Washington Park neighborhood.
>
> The cause of death was determined to be a single gunshot wound in the head which

was not self-inflicted. Time of death is estimated at one week to ten days prior to discovery of the body. Police are continuing to investigate what they believe is a homicide.

This is a continuing story.

Written By
Rick Hughes
Rick covers the city and county of Albany for the Times Union. Reach him at

Once again, Boone wondered why the article's reference to the New Karner Road post office rang a distant bell in his mind. He looked up from the paper, thinking to ask Marianne about the post office as she stepped into his office. Before he could say anything, she told him Marilyn Creekson was on the office line. She wanted to speak with him. He grabbed the phone.

"Boone here."

"Mr. Boone? This is Marilyn Creekson."

He waited a moment in case she wanted to continue speaking. When she didn't, he said, "Thanks for calling. How can I help you?"

"I want to apologize for my rudeness on Tuesday. You caught me by surprise, I guess. It was wrong of me to, . . . well, you know. But," she sighed, "I have to ask, did you mean what you said? That you were investigating the murder of my son, as well as that girl?"

"Yes," he answered. "I said that, and I mean it. I don't work for you, but I believe whoever murdered your son was involved with the murder of my client's friend."

"How did she die? That girl?"

"Drug overdose, I believe. Someone gave her an opioid laced with fentanyl, which put her into cardiac arrest. According to those who knew her well, she never experimented with drugs."

Marilyn was quiet for a minute.

"May I ask who your client is?"

"I'm sorry, but I really can't say much beyond the fact that my client is, . . . was, a friend of Geraldine Bronson."

As he spoke, he felt a little jolt of adrenaline as the significance of the New Karner Road post office, which had seemed just beyond his grasp, began to make sense. It was significant, because . . . because, . . .

". . . if it will help," she said, breaking his chain of thought.

"Sorry, I was interrupted," he said, upset that whatever the connection was with the New Karner Road post office, it had just slipped away. "What was that?"

"I said that I will speak with you if it will help. Would you like me to come to your office?"

"Whatever is most convenient for you is fine with me," he said, bringing up his weekly calendar on his display.

"Tomorrow then," she said. "What time?"

Glancing at his display, he said, "Ten, but any time really."

"Ten it is then," she said. "See you then."

"Thank you. Bye now."

Her 'goodbye' was barely a whisper before ending the call.

He hung up the phone, and with a raised voice, asked, "Marianne. New Karner Road post office. Why does that seem important to me?"

She got up from her desk and stood in the doorway between their offices. "No reason that I can think of," she said, "Except that Abe Creekson may have a post office box there."

"Oh," he said, disappointed. "Probably just a coincidence then. Thanks."

"Seems to me, I remember you saying something very different about coincidences," she said.

"And that was?"

"That you didn't believe in them. Remember? We were at my parents' house in Ballston Spa."

"I know. But that was different. Some things are too obvious to be just a coincidence."

"So, there are fake coincidences, and then there are genuine coincidences? Seriously?"

"No. I didn't mean that, . . . I guess what I'm saying is that I don't see any relationship between where this body was discovered and Mr. Creekson's post office box."

"That kid they found behind the post office, you mean?"

"Yeah. Itzy had put me in touch with him. He was David Creekson's dealer, remember?"

"So, where the murdered body of David Creekson's dealer was found, behind the same post office where Abe Creekson has a post office box, . . . there's no connection?"

He leaned back in his chair, his lips pressed tightly together as he considered her question.

"Shit! You're right," he exclaimed, feeling embarrassed that he hadn't drawn out that link on his own.

At the time, when the dealer had asked him, "You're talking about David, right?" he hadn't grasped the significance of the question. *Why would the dealer want to know* **which** *Creekson unless he was also dealing with another one? The father?*

"I'm sure you would have figured it out," she said before turning around to go back to her desk, whispering to herself, "some day."

Going to the Albany *whitepages.com*, he quickly confirmed there were only two listings for Creeksons in the Albany area. Abraham and Marilyn.

EIGHT

Friday morning, Boone took more care with his work attire for Marilyn Creekson's appointment. It wasn't every day he questioned the mother of a teen-aged murder victim. Thinking back over his career with the New York State Police, he remembered being tasked with seeking information from family members after the death of a young person. But none of those cases involved a deliberate taking of life.

As he tied and re-tied his tie before deciding to go without it, he recalled his conversation with Marilyn three days earlier, brief as it was, putting her animosity down to grief. After all, she had buried her son the previous weekend. That she called him later to apologize and agree to speak with him was encouraging. He looked forward to a productive day.

At the office, he straightened up his side of the office, cleared off his desk except for a legal pad, and made a fresh pot of coffee. Marianne organized her side of the office as well. Boone was pleased to see she had dressed professionally, instead of her usual jeans and casual tops.

As the time for her appointment approached, he ducked into the men's room for a quick rinse with mouthwash. Opening the door to head back to the office, Marilyn was just passing in the hall.

"Good morning," he said.

She smiled briefly and shrugged as she walked. Wearing a vintage shirtwaist dress with short sleeves, no jewelry or makeup, she looked much older than her age.

He asked her if she wanted anything like coffee, tea, or juice. She declined. Stepping ahead, he opened the office door for her. She walked in, looked around briefly, and took one of the client chairs in front of his desk. She sat her purse on the floor next to the chair.

After shutting the door, Boone went behind his desk to sit. Marianne stepped over to the door separating the two sides of the office, and said quietly, "I'll shut this for you."

Marilyn turned her head halfway towards Marianne and nodded but said nothing in response. When she turned to face Boone, he said, "That was Marianne Bell, my assistant."

She asked, "Is she a private investigator as well?"

"No, at least not for now. She's only been here a month or two."

"Oh."

He reached into his pocket for his pen.

"Are you going to record this?" she asked.

"I hadn't planned to," he said. "Did you want me to?"

"No."

"I don't have a problem if you want to record this with your phone."

"No, I'd rather not."

"Well then," he said, "let's get started."

"Okay." She fixed her gaze on a window behind his desk.

"Why don't you tell me about your son," he asked.

"What do you want to know?" She continued looking towards the window, not at him.

"Can you tell me what kind of person was he?"

She leaned back in her chair and looked even further off into the distance, a smile playing on her lips.

"He was a sweet child when he was little," she said. "Very sensitive, but not a baby, if you know what I mean."

Her eyes flitted towards Boone, then returned to the window.

"He didn't carry on if he skinned his knee or got bumped while roughhousing with his father. But if I became upset over something, he would be very concerned and try in his own way to comfort me. I had to do my best not to cry over anything around him, it disturbed him so much."

Looking down at her hands clasped in her lap, she continued.

"He wasn't a 'mama's boy' though. He was close to his father as a child. They were always going somewhere together."

"Like where?"

Sighing, she looked out the window. He was thinking she wanted to unburden herself, but without actually acknowledging another person was in the room. It reminded him of Jitter's remarks about David, wanting to have sex without being present for it.

"Oh, sometimes my husband would take David to his office on weekends, or to different places, like a movie, or . . . I don't know. Just out. Sometimes, I would worry because they would sometimes be out late on school nights when David got older."

"So, he was a happy as a child and a teenager?"

She looked at Boone, her eyes narrowing a bit. "No. Not always," she said. "As a teen, he would become sometimes withdrawn. He still went out with his father, but it seemed more like he didn't want to, as if it was a sacrifice. Oh, I suppose he wanted to talk with his friends on the phone, or go out with them, that's only normal.

"And as my husband's work became more demanding over time, there seemed to be some tension developing between them. Abe would want David to spend time with him, but David didn't seem to be interested. Sometimes, I felt like a referee."

"Did your son have any girlfriends as he grew up?"

She looked around and fidgeted with her hands before answering. "I'm not sure. He would go out on dates, but there was never anyone special. He went out with them once, or rarely twice, but no."

She unexpectedly chuckled and, for a moment, looked at Boone.

"I sometimes suspected he was entertaining them at home whenever my husband and I were out. Between his work, and my involvement with so many charities, we had more social engagements than I would have liked."

"Can you tell me anything about your husband?"

She took in a deep breath and sighed as she exhaled. "He's a very busy man. I hardly see him anymore. I was only twenty-seven when we married. He was forty."

Again, she looked out the window, but with more concentration. "I think his energy, his drive to succeed, impressed me, and of course he was already successful by that point. It didn't take much for him to woo me away from what I was doing. Sometimes, I almost wish, . . . " her voice trailed off.

"How soon after you were married was David born?"

"Two years." She glanced nervously at the door separating his office from Marianne's, and lowered her voice, saying, "I probably shouldn't be telling you this, but . . . "

He leaned forward, holding his pen, ready to take notes.

"Please," she said, "don't write this down. This is just between us, and I don't want there ever to be any record of what I'm about to tell you."

He laid his pen down. "If it helps," he said, "I promise not to write this down or make a note of it later."

She leaned forward, gripping the forward edge of his desk with one hand, and looked directly at him.

"Abe is not David's father," she whispered.

"Does your husband know this?" he asked.

"I'm not sure. I think he suspects it, since we had no children after David. Not that he ever seems interested in me anymore. We have separate bedrooms. We only see each other when we have to entertain one of his clients at the club, or a charity event. Like I said, he is a very, very busy man."

As much as Boone wanted to ask who David's father was, he thought it better to let her be the one to offer such information. He looked at her, saying nothing. She looked down at her hands, now clasped tightly in her lap.

She looked away and out the window. "I've never told anyone that before. You should feel special."

"Thank you," he said, even as he wondered why she even thought to mention it.

"I just thought," she said before hesitating, "I should tell *someone*. It's a lot to carry around. I've never even told David's father, who knows my husband well."

"Listen, I know this may be difficult for you, but can you tell me what was going on at the house that night, you know, the night that, . . ."

"I know what you mean," she said.

She took in a deep breath, as if to collect herself.

"I had gone to bed early shortly after dinner. I wasn't feeling well, so I took an

Ambien to help me sleep. My husband was working late in his home office."

At this moment, scarcely able to breathe, Boone laid his pen down next to his legal pad, wanting to concentrate on what she said next and how she said it.

"I knew David was having some friend over that evening. I didn't know it was a girl. At least I can't remember now if I knew it. I think if I knew he was entertaining a young lady, I would have made it a point to stay up, at least to meet her."

Again, looking out the window, she continued. "I sometimes wonder how things would have turned out if I had stayed up."

As she spoke, Boone began making notes in his own version of shorthand.

She grimaced and shook her head. "I don't remember how much later it was when I heard a lot of commotion outside my bedroom door. Abe was yelling. There were lots of people in the hall, and I was quite drowsy from the Ambien."

"I got up, pulled on a robe and stepped into the hall. There were so many people there. I could see a police officer taking a girl down the stairs. The girl had some sort of coat over her shoulders. Her legs were bare, and . . . I don't know how I knew she was undressed, but I knew."

"Abe was crying, and some ambulance people were, . . . " her voice broke, and she reached into her purse for a handkerchief. Boone opened his bottom desk drawer, pulled out a box of tissues, and slid it across the desk toward her. She shook her head as she wiped her nose.

Eventually, she was able to speak the words, ". . . wheeling my son's body, . . . " before breaking down and crying softly, by then making no effort to stem the tears streaming down her cheeks. "I'm sorry," she said, speaking without seeing. "I'm so, so sorry."

He knew she was apologizing to her dead son, not to him.

After a few minutes, she blotted her face with her handkerchief, blew her nose gently, and said, "There isn't much more to tell you. They wouldn't let me see his room where, . . . you know. For the next few days, I was simply a basket case."

"I was on tranquilizers for the funeral. In fact, the only thing I remember clearly was seeing you standing to one side behind the tent, and wondering who you were, and why you were there."

"I have to ask," he said, "did anyone make any effort to fill in the blanks for you later?"

"I wouldn't let them. Nothing could bring David back, so what was the point? Abe told me he heard the girl screaming from downstairs. He ran upstairs to see what the problem was and found, . . . whatever he found. I know he spoke at length later with the police. Some woman detective said they would keep us informed. Later, they told my husband that since their only suspect had died, they were closing the file."

She looked exhausted, her eyes red-rimmed, and her chin trembling. He knew she had reached her limit in talking about her son.

"To be honest," she said, "I'm thinking of leaving my husband. I can barely stand to be in that house, and he's either working at the office, or at home, or God knows where. Maybe it's his way of dealing with it, but . . . "

Although Boone already knew the answer, he asked, "Do you think your husband might speak with me?"

She looked at him. "You're joking, of course. He hardly speaks to me, and we live in the same house!" Looking off to one side, she added, "I will let him know I spoke with you, if that's all right."

"Tell him please, to call me if he has any questions," Boone replied. He waited a moment to give her an opportunity to say anything if she felt like it.

Finally, to break the silence, which was becoming uncomfortable, he said, "I know this has been difficult for you. Are you sure I can't get you something?"

She raised her face, sniffed, and said, "You know, that coffee smells good, but . . . no. No thank you. I feel the need to leave. No offense."

"None taken. I can step outside the office to give you some privacy for a few minutes, if that would help?"

"No. That's not necessary. I have just one request."

"Name it."

"If, . . . no, I think *when* sounds better, . . . when you find out anything about who was behind my son's murder, you'll tell me? I think I'm ready to hear the truth now."

"You can count on it," he said.

"Good," she said, reaching down to collect her purse. "Please don't take too long."

After she had left, Boone looked over his notes, adding details that he hadn't time to jot down as they spoke. He had conducted probably thousands of interviews with witnesses, victims, and suspects over his decades in law enforcement. This was the first time his subject seemed indifferent to the process. Speak, or don't speak, it was all the same to her.

NINE

MONDAY MORNING, BOONE WAS early to work. Over the weekend, he had developed a line of approach on the Creekson file, and wanted to bring his client, Clive Townsend, up to date. And to pick the man's brain while he was at it. But like all plans born of enthusiasm early in the day, Boone's strategy collapsed before the workday even began.

As he was picking up his handset to call Clive, Marianne interrupted him.

"A Nick Grimme is on line one for you," she said. "He is a partner in Hirschhorn Enterprises."

He must have looked confused, so she added, "Remember Judith Hirschhorn?"

As Boone quickly reached for the console to connect with the caller, she said, "I thought so, wuss!"

"Boone here," he answered, thinking, *Marianne always knows what to say.*

"Carl Boone, detective, I understand." The voice was a mild tenor with no discernible accent.

"Yes."

"Carl, my name is Nicholas Grimme, but you can call me Nick."

"Okay, Mr. Grimme. I prefer Boone, or Detective Boone. At least until I get to know you. How can I help you?"

"Sorry. All right, *de-tect-ive*. I believe you know my partner's wife, Judith Hirschhorn. Am I right?"

"Yes. I've met with her." To make certain there was no misunderstanding, he added, "Once. In the office."

Grimme laughed. "I get you. I understand she may have hired you to investigate me. Is that correct?"

"She has not hired me to do anything. How did you come by that idea?"

"Judith is, well, . . . she's kind of fragile, and we keep track of her comings and goings." Grimme said. "She sometimes comes up with weird conspiracy theories. But listen. We sometimes need a gumshoe. Anyway, . . . "

"Anyone interested in hiring us usually refers to us as a private investigator."

"Look. I'm sorry, sometimes I let my mouth get away from me. I don't mean to piss you off. We just, from time to time, need help in that area. Is this anything you are interested in?"

"Depends on the case," Boone said.

"Depends on the case," Grimme repeated in a dragged-out monotone. "Okay. I have a case right now that would benefit by someone with your talents. When can I meet with you?"

"How about later today? Say, around two o'clock? Does that work for you?"

"I'll be there," Grimme said.

"See you then," Boone said, hanging up, wondering if he was going to regret it.

After texting the details on the appointment to Marianne, he called Clive Townsend. He had to leave a message. Clive's secretary informed Boone that, "Mr. Townsend is in court."

Not three minutes later, his iPhone signaled an incoming call. He looked at the display, which read, '**C.Townsend**.'

He answered, "Boone here."

"You called?"

"Yeah. Where are you?"

"In the hall, outside Supreme Court, waiting my turn on a motion."

"Don't you have to be inside to hear your name?"

Townsend snorted. "I'm so far down the fucking calendar, it'll be the Second Coming before they get to me. What did you want?"

"Just to bring you up to date on the Creekson file and bounce a few things off you."

"Lunch tomorrow?"

"Sure. Where?"

"The Chambers. Eleven-thirty."

"See you then." He ended the call.

Now what? He made a pot of coffee.

* * *

The morning passed without incident, and Boone left for lunch. As always, he asked Marianne if he could bring anything back for her, and as always, she declined. She would take lunch in the kitchenette with something she brought in from her apartment.

She lived on State Street in a brownstone overlooking Washington Park, less than four blocks from the office, and walked to work during mild weather. He knew he should follow her example, take lighter lunches, and adopt a more regular gym schedule. But he also knew he wouldn't.

That afternoon, Nick Grimme of Hirschhorn Enterprises knocked twice on the doorframe and walked through the open door on Boone's side of the office.

"Detective Boone?" he asked.

Boone looked up to see Gig Young's doppelgänger. Grimme was clean shaven and Brylcreamed, in lightweight gray slacks, navy blazer, pinstriped button-down and navy club tie. He could not see this man, who looked like a clean-cut actor in a sixties romantic comedy, as a pornographer. And, if Judith Hirschhorn was right, an extortionist.

"The same," Boone answered, standing up behind his desk and extending his hand. Grimme gave him a vigorous two-handed shake before sitting down.

"So, this is your place," Grimme said, casually slipping one of his business cards out of his pocket and putting it on Boone's desk, snapping the corner as he did so.

"Pretty much," Boone said, picking up the card and putting it in his top desk drawer. "Coffee?"

"No thanks. I just have a few minutes to tell you what we need."

"Okay. Your first conference is free, and I only charge half on discovering my first clue."

Grimme smiled at the joke. "First," he said, "I have to ask, are you aware of what Hirschhorn Enterprises does?"

"Why don't you tell me?"

"We produce adult videos which we distribute online and through certain retail outlets that some would consider pornographic. We also publish magazines and distribute merchandise designed to enhance the sexual experience for individuals and as couples."

"That was pretty much my understanding," Boone said.

"So, do you have any problem working for us?"

"As long as I don't have to do anything on camera, or anything illegal, no. At least not for now."

Grimme chuckled. He glanced at the closed door separating Marianne's work area from Boone's office before asking, "What do you think about pornography?"

"As little as possible."

"Not a fan, then?"

"It's not that. I used to be an avid consumer, but that was back in the days of Playboy and Hustler, which today would be considered, I don't know, . . . what? Soft core?"

Grimme smiled. "That's for sure. Actually, the stuff in the old Playboy now shows up in ads. But you're not a fan of today's, ah, . . . shall we say, variety of pornography?"

"No. I believe it degrades the viewer as much, if not more, than the performer."

"Understood. Well, that being said, we supply a product that many self-respecting adults want to purchase."

Even though he thought that no adult seeking hard-core pornography could consider himself a self-respecting anything, Boone simply nodded.

"We have one customer in particular that has very specific tastes which we try to cater to. The customer can't use an online account for various reasons to do with privacy issues and does not wish to be seen entering or leaving from one of our retail locations. So, we have an arrangement where we deliver a package to this customer from time to time and charge their credit card through ACH."

"You're referring to Automated Clearing House transactions, correct?" Boone said.

"Yes. Anyway, if you handle these deliveries for us, we will notify your office of the time and place of the delivery and pay you five hundred dollars per delivery. Is that something you are willing to undertake?"

Boone tilted his head back and looked at Grimme through half-lidded eyes before answering, thinking, *This customer must pay a bucket load for this content!*

"Why not have him simply rent a post office box and mail your stuff to the customer?"

Grimme opened his mouth as if to speak and closed it. After a brief hesitation, he said, "The Postal Service sometimes opens packages being forwarded by our retail locations in cooperation with the U.S. Attorney's office. We'd rather avoid such situations."

"What kind of material would . . . oh. You deal in child pornography?"

"Never," Grimme said. "All of our models are of legal age, although I admit some of them look much younger than their years. So, are you willing to handle this for us?"

"You can't just have it delivered to his house or e-mail it?"

"Again, there are privacy issues. The customer does not live alone."

"Why don't you just drop off your own package?"

"Sometimes it's inconvenient. But we feel involving a professional third party, such as yourself, is probably the safest, most secure way to go."

"I don't know. It just doesn't make much sense to me."

"Try it once and see what you think. If you don't like it, that's up to you."

"I suppose I could give it a shot," Boone said. "So long as it works with my schedule, and it's local."

"Oh, that won't be a problem," Grimme said. "Your first delivery will be this coming Saturday. I'll have the package, with delivery instructions and a check delivered here by Thursday afternoon. And we'll see how it goes. Okay?"

"Look," Boone said. "Like you say, this will be a one-off. If it works out, I'll want you to sign one of my 'scope of services' agreements for any long-term relationship. Does that work?"

"It does. Frankly, it would surprise me if you didn't want some kind of agreement going forward."

"Then we understand each other," Boone said.

"We do."

They shook hands, and Grimme left the office. Boone opened a client file on his desktop and made some notes on the client and the proposed engagement. He looked down the hall to confirm Grimme was gone. Once satisfied, he went to the men's room to wash his hands, wondering if he had just descended into the same category of bottom dwellers as the disgraced Michael Avenatti, known as 'the creepy porn lawyer' by some.

* * *

Wednesday morning, Boone told Marianne he would be having lunch with Townsend to update him on the Creekson file.

She made a little pout before saying, "That's what I meant when I said I wanted to be more involved in what we do here."

"The reason I told you," he replied, "was because I think you should come along. It's only fair, since a lot of what we know comes from your online research."

She brightened. "Now you're talking!"

"But, until then, I'd like you to dig deeper on Geraldine's parents. I want to know as much as there is to know before I speak with them."

"Can I come along with that as well?" she asked.

"Let's see how comfortable they are with me first, okay?"

"You're the boss!"

He nodded and went into his office, not feeling very much like the boss of anything.

* * *

After locking the office, the pair walked down the hill to Chambers Bar and Grille shortly after eleven to meet with Clive Townsend.

Fifteen minutes later, they arrived, with Boone wishing they had driven. Shorter though she was, Marianne had set a blistering pace to the restaurant. He was grateful for the air conditioning once inside.

Clive was standing at the large entrance to the back seating area. He waved them towards him. As always, he was perfectly attired in a navy pinstripe two-piece suit, brilliant white button-down shirt with a red power tie, and highly polished cap toe dress shoes. Boone wondered how he managed it, having a fourteen-year-old daughter, and being the senior partner in his firm, not to mention a staggering case load.

Once the three were seated and their drinks ordered, Boone started to introduce Marianne when Clive interrupted him.

"I know this young lady, and Miss Bell, it's nice to see you again. You look much better than our last meeting."

She blushed at his courtliness, especially his use of the old-fashioned appellation, 'Miss.'

"Thank you, Mr. Townsend."

"Clive, please."

The waitress arrived to bring their drinks and lunch orders. After she left, Townsend turned to Boone and asked, "So Shamus, what do you have for me?"

Boone answered, "Marianne and I are both convinced your daughter's friend is as much an innocent victim as David Creekson."

"Tell me something I don't already know," Townsend growled.

"We believe both murders were carried out by someone close to the couple, possibly one of David's parents. Personally, I suspect the father is involved, but . . . "

"Why not the mother?" Townsend asked.

"I've spoken with her," Boone said. "She is devastated over her son's death. That night, she had gone to her bedroom after dinner, not feeling well, and had taken a sleeping pill. She tells me she knew her son had a friend coming over but did not know it was a girl. According to her, the father was working late in his home office when he heard Geraldine upstairs screaming, He ran upstairs, found David stabbed and bleeding out, and dialed nine-one-one."

Townsend asked him, "Did the mother hear anyone screaming?"

"No. She was told about that by the father."

Boone took a long sip of his ice water before continuing.

"Hearing the commotion, she went out into the hall to find her husband excited and upset, a police officer escorting the girl downstairs, and her son's body being wheeled out. She did not see the crime scene, and was only told later that, with Geraldine's death, the police were closing their file. She is emotionally drained and tells me she plans to leave her husband at some point."

At that point, the waitress delivered their lunch orders. Townsend and Boone both ordered sandwiches, Townsend's with fries. In a nod towards improving his diet, Boone went with Cole slaw. Marianne's side salad with oil and vinegar on the side looked diminutive compared to their sandwiches.

"What about the husband, Abe?" Townsend asked around a mouth full of corned beef.

"Marianne did the research on him, so I'll let her take over," Boone said, nodding in her direction, and picking up his pastrami on rye.

Beaming, Marianne started off saying, "I will not bore you with information already publicly known about Mr. Creekson. The most significant things I have discovered are, first, he has a separate bank account with HSBC in his name alone, with an average daily balance of four to five thousand dollars."

"He takes out cash withdrawals of several hundred dollars every week to ten days from this account. Second, he has informed delivery on mail addressed to their home, which revealed nothing unusual. *But* he has an individual post office box at the New Karner Road Post Office. No idea what it's used for."

She leaned forward, and in a lowered voice, said, "I got into one of his credit reports online, but don't see any indication he has bills or creditor mail sent to that box."

With his eyebrows raised and the corners of his mouth turned down in an exaggerated frown, Townsend nodded.

"Third," she said, "he runs a tab every ten days to two weeks at the Waterworks Pub, . . . "

"That's a gay bar, isn't it?" Townsend interrupted.

"It is," she continued. "Also, he donates to the Republican Party under his name, but he donates two to three times as much to Democrat Party PACs, which don't have to reveal their donors. So, he can look like a GOP supporter, but in reality, . . . "

"The sonofabitch is actually a Democrat!" Townsend said. "I'll be dipped."

"Last, and this is interesting, David Creekson's dealer was recently murdered and dumped behind the New Karner Road Post Office, which neither of us believes to be mere coincidence. And we think David's dealer may have been dealing with David's father."

"So, now what?" Townsend asked.

"This puzzle is coming together," Boone said, "but there is a large piece I can't quite figure out. I know that Abe Creekson is part of it. I'd love to see what kind of mail he's receiving in his post office box. But given that the Albany PD is no longer interested in the case, I can't figure out a way to do that."

"Do you have the box number?" Townsend asked.

"Yes," Marianne piped up. "Box number 2790."

"Let me give that some thought," Townsend said. "As a law office authorized to issue legal process, we can get a street address for a post office box. Of course, that still won't tell us what kind of mail he's getting there."

Turning to Boone, he said, "What are your plans going forward?"

"I'm going to ask Marianne to creep Geraldine's parents, so I know more about them than they do before I go to talk with them. I'll have to see what they have to offer before deciding on next steps."

"Well," Townsend grumbled, "keep me posted. I'll see what I can do with the post office box."

By the time they had finished with lunch, Clive had managed to eat his entire sandwich, along with most of his fries. Boone could barely struggle through half of his sandwich, and barely touched his slaw. Marianne left only the two dinner rolls on her bread-and-butter plate.

Clive picked up the tab and, after exchanging goodbyes with Boone and Marianne, went out the rear entrance into the hall for the elevator up to his floor of the building. Standing up, Boone patted his stomach, again wishing they had driven down the hill, knowing the office was uphill all the way back.

"Ready?" she asked.

"As I'll ever be," Boone said. "Lead on, and if I fall behind, don't wait for me."

TEN

MARIANNE REACHED THE OFFICE ahead of Boone. He took the elevator to their floor instead of walking up the single flight of stairs. By the time he reached the office and unlocked the door to his side, he could see Marianne already absorbed in her most recent assignment, 'creeping,' as she called it, Geraldine's parents.

After opening the windows behind his desk, he sat down, wishing he had followed her example and had something lighter for lunch. Even better, he needed a nap. He opened the top right-hand desk drawer where he kept his 1911 Colt .45 semi-auto and shoulder rig. Then he leaned back in his chair and parked his feet on a corner of the drawer.

Forty minutes later, he heard, "Boss? Boss! You awake?"

Without opening his eyes, he said, "I was just deep in thought."

"Uh huh," she said. "Here's the scoop, what there is of it, on the Russell's."

He dropped his feet to the floor and sat up. "The Russell's?"

"Geraldine's parents."

"Yeah. Anything interesting?"

"Not really. Hard working middle-class people, not even so much as a speeding ticket. Looks like they were trying to do everything right."

She laid a two-page printout on his desk and returned to her office. Boone picked it up and scanned it, only to see that Marianne was spot on. There was nothing to suggest anything unusual or suspicious on the part of either of Geraldine's parents. Looking at the information on their work schedules, he figured the coming weekend would be as good a time as any to approach them.

THE FOLLOWING afternoon, a local courier service dropped off a letter-sized manila wrapper containing what felt like several sheets of stiff paper. Taped to the top was a smaller envelope from Hirschhorn Enterprises addressed to Boone. He opened the envelope to read the following.

Dear Mr. Boone:

Attached is your first delivery for our client. Please place the package on the north bench in the central area of Lafayette Park at precisely 1:15 in the afternoon of Saturday, May 22. The weather forecast is optimal. After placing the package, leave the area as quickly as possible. Our customer is very skittish when it comes to possible surveillance. Payment is enclosed, as agreed. Trusting in your discretion, I remain,

Nick Grimme

He laid the check to one side. Turning the package over, he could see the flap had been sealed with an old-fashioned red wax seal to ensure it was unopened prior to delivery. He shook his head in disbelief.

This is stupid. It has to be a joke, he thought. *Why set up something with an excellent chance of failure? What if someone not involved is already sitting on the bench? What if some third party gets to the package before the customer?* He could think of several locations in the immediate area that would work better for such a handoff. *What's wrong with a day use rental locker like the ones at the downtown bus terminal?*

Does Grimme have some other purpose in mind? He wondered if someone else employed by Hirschhorn Enterprises would be there to watch how he handled the drop off. *Am I being set up?*

He was having second thoughts about becoming a delivery service for Hirschhorn Enterprises. There was something about them, and Grimme especially, that left him feeling uncomfortable. He left early for the day and hit the gym on his way home. He did his best thinking on tactics and strategy during a strenuous workout.

* * *

Saturday morning dawned clear, with temperature in the upper sixties and low humidity. If Boone were still a runner, it would have been a perfect morning for a five-mile jog. But his knees and ankles no longer tolerated running on pavement, or anything else. As it was, he went for a brisk three-mile walk before breakfast. Feeling virtuous afterwards, he allowed himself some orange marmalade on his toast.

After dressing in a pair of dockers, a polo shirt and boat shoes, and a light windbreaker to hide his shoulder rig, he made his way to the office to meet with Marianne. Leaving a package on a park bench in the afternoon, and not being allowed to remain in the area to ensure pickup, left things too much to chance. He enlisted Marianne in the delivery. As far as he knew, Grimme had never seen her before, and a second pair of eyes might come in handy.

The plan was for her to sit on a nearby bench with a paperback before the designated time, and simply watch. He would make the delivery and leave the area as instructed.

Lafayette Park lay on the north side of the New York State Capitol. A small park, its main feature was a fountain in the center of the park, surrounded by a circular walk and four stone benches on the walk's circumference.

At quarter to one, Marianne took her seat on the east park bench, opened her paperback, and pretended to read. Wearing sunglasses under her ball cap, she could maintain close observation of the north bench without appearing to pay it any attention.

At one thirteen, Boone walked slowly into the park from the north side. There were very few people in the park. He sat down on the north bench, placing the package next to him.

Bending down and pretending to tie one of his shoelaces, he then stood up and walked casually through the park towards the south entrance. He made it a point not to turn around or give any sign that he might have an interest in who showed up to take the package. Less than ten minutes later, he was back in the office.

Five minutes after that, Marianne arrived. Entering through his door, she said, "You'll never guess who picked up the package."

"No. Anyone you recognized?"

She handed him her phone, already opened to the Photos app. "Here," she said. "I got photos. See for yourself."

Boone looked at the first photo. A tall woman in a long, lightweight trench coat sat down next to the envelope. With her large sunglasses and headscarf, her features were difficult to make out. In the second photo, she had picked up the envelope. In the third photo, she was breaking the seal on the back flap.

In the fourth photo, she was looking at the top of a sheet of paper, maybe a photograph. From her expression, she appeared to be upset, even alarmed. In the fifth and final photo, she had removed her sunglasses to wipe something away from one of her eyes. Tears, perhaps?

At first, Boone did not understand why Grimme would have him delivering pornographic material to Judith Hirschhorn. "What the hell?" he said.

"How does it feel to be played?" Marianne asked.

"Not good," he said. "Not good at all."

Working cases as a private investigator was very different from his days as a sworn law enforcement officer. He had more latitude, but also more exposure to actors with goals and interests not always obvious. He was going to have to trust his instincts more than he had with Grimme.

Grimme had done a masterful job in trying to conflict him out of helping Judith. But all he had accomplished was convincing Boone that Judith's fears were legitimate. He also came to realize the personal degradation for a porn star was lifelong, regardless of what they thought when they made that initial decision to expose themselves and perform sex on film.

He opened his top desk drawer, took out the check from Hirschhorn Enterprises and tore it in half. Holding it towards Marianne, he said, "Send this back to Mr. Grimme, would you?"

She slowly shook her head. "You're not supposed to know who picked up this stuff, are you?"

"No. You're right. Okay, just shred it. See how long he takes to ask me if I'm going to cash his check. And if he calls, I'm not in, you'll take a message."

"What about Judith? What if she calls back?"

"Give her an appointment," he said. "Maybe next time, she'll tell me the truth."

She picked up the two pieces of the check. "When are you going to talk to the Russell's?"

"I think tomorrow afternoon is probably better."

"Can I come along?"

"No. I think it will be hard enough for them to accept me showing up to talk about their daughter. Two people might be too much. But, if I need to go back, I'll mention that I want to bring my assistant along. Okay?"

She shrugged. "You're the boss."

* * *

The Russells' home on Brockley Drive was a white colonial on a half-acre lot. Younger trees shaded one side and the back of the lot.

When Boone pulled up in front, a man he recognized as Stanley Russell from the funeral was operating a riding mower close to the street. A woman, with her back to the road, was tending to plantings in front of the house.

Boone turned off the ignition and stepped out of his car. Russell shut off his mower and walked over to Boone's car on the passenger side.

"Can I help you?" he asked.

Boone walked around the front of his car and held out one of his business cards. "I hope so."

Russell took the card and glanced at it. "A private investigator, huh? What are you investigating?"

"The father of one of your daughter's friends has asked me, . . . "

"Hold up there," Russell said. "We've already been through all this with the police. They pinned that boy's death on our daughter and, . . ." he looked down, shook his head, and raised his head to look at Boone, said, "Please leave."

Elaine Russell had left her garden bed and Boone could see her coming up behind her husband, her eyebrows knitted together. As she approached, she pulled off her gardening gloves.

"Mr. Russell," Boone said, loudly enough for her to hear, "we believe your daughter was not responsible for David Creekson's death. She was an innocent victim of whoever carried this out. I'm just trying to develop evidence to get the police to look more deeply into, . . ."

"I don't see how we can possibly help you. We don't know anything about what took place in that house. Can't you just leave us alone?"

"Stan, what does he want?" Elaine asked.

Turning his head slightly to speak to her, Russell said, "He says he's investigating Gerry's death and thinks she didn't kill that boy, and . . ."

"Shouldn't we at least talk to him?" she asked.

Still looking at Boone, but speaking to his wife, Russell said, "No! We don't need to talk to this guy and bring all that up again. There's nothing we can tell him that will make make any difference in what the police have decided."

Boone tried again. "Mr. Russell, I just want to get a sense of what kind of person your daughter was. You never know what little bit of information will lead me, or any investigator, towards other information that might make a difference in the outcome."

His eyes shining, Russell said, "You'll be wasting your time with us. Why don't you talk with that boy's family?"

"I already have," Boone quickly replied. "At least with his mother, and from what she tells me, I'm convinced your daughter is innocent. I don't want to cause you any distress. Won't you help us?"

"Who's your client?"

"A friend of your daughter. She's very upset, and her father has asked me to look into this on her behalf."

"But you won't tell me who?"

"I'm sorry, but without their permission, . . . "

"Stanley, just let him ask his questions, and if we feel they're out of line, can't we just, . . . "

"Fine!" Russell yelled, throwing Boone's card to the ground. "You can talk to him if you want!" He turned away from her and walked back to the lawn mower. He didn't get on the mower, but stood next to it, one hand gripping the edge of the seatback. His shoulders heaved as he wept.

Glancing at her husband, and then at Boone, Elaine said, "Look. You've come at a bad time is all. My husband is still trying to come to grips with losing our daughter." She bent down and picked up Boone's card.

"How about I call your office and we can get together another time?"

Realizing that was probably all he would get out of the Russell's, he said, "That would be fine. I appreciate it very much."

Elaine nodded. Turning away from Boone, she stepped quickly over to her husband's side.

Boone could hear her speaking softly to her husband as he walked back around to the driver's side of his car. After starting the car, he looked at the Russell home. Stanley was still standing next to the mower while Elaine slowly rubbed her husband's back as she spoke to him.

Thinking, *Nice work, Boone!* he headed for his apartment. He wondered how long it might take Geraldine's mother to call for an appointment to talk with him.

ELEVEN

IT WAS JUST BEFORE lunch on Monday when someone knocked forcefully on Boone's office door. Murf had finally gotten around to installing a solid door between the two areas and having a 'No Entry' sign posted on Marianne's hall door, along with 'Carl Boone, Private Investigator' along with 'Hours by Appointment Only' painted in gold leaf on Boone's door. Until then, people had been walking into Marianne's office, which sometimes unsettled her.

"Come in," Boone yelled.

The door opened slowly, and a man the size of Boise, Idaho walked through it, a toothpick sticking out of one side of his mouth. His three-day beard growth looked like a wire brush fashioned from silver. Wearing a faded porkpie hat, a short-sleeved polo that was at least two sizes too small under a light jacket, and well-worn jeans, he looked anything but prosperous. Boone couldn't see the man's feet and doubted his visitor could either. He wondered how he tied his shoes.

"Can I help you?"

"You're Carl Boone, the private eye?"

"Yes."

Something about the man's stance and attitude stopped Boone from offering him a business card. Instead, he casually pulled open the top right-hand desk drawer where he kept his Colt semi-automatic.

When the man didn't say anything, Boone tried again. "Can I help you with anything? Or do you plan to stand there all day?"

The man put his right hand inside the pocket of his jacket. Boone could clearly see the outline of a small handgun in the man's fist. He made it out to be a snub-nosed revolver. Reaching inside his open desk drawer, he carefully laid the Colt on his desk.

"I'll bet mine has more bullets than yours," he said.

"Yeah. Maybe so." The man slowly removed his hand from his pocket. Boone was relieved to see it was empty.

"I just wanted to tell you to lay off this business with the Creekson family."

"Sorry, but I don't work for them, and I don't take orders from them."

"Well, you better start," the man said.

"Or what? You gonna teach me a lesson?"

The man took the toothpick out of his mouth and said, "You don't want to wind up behind the New Karner Road post office, now do ya?"

The mention of the New Karner Road post office grabbed Boone's attention. He knew that hit men tended to be greedy, incompetent, and more often than not, were police informants. But every so often, one came along that knew his business. He wasn't sure where this man landed on the continuum between blowhard and killer. But there was no pressing need to figure that out in the moment.

Boone stood up and said, "Tell Abe I send my regards, and that I'll be seeing him very soon. Okay?"

"I didn't say nothin' about Mr. Creekson," the man said. "And you're a smartass."

"But self effacing," Boone replied.

A look of confusion passed over the man's face. "You been warned," he said, and left with the door swinging widely behind him.

Now what? Boone wondered.

Marianne opened the door between their offices.

"I heard someone talking. Who was that?"

"No one important," he said, deciding not to mention the thug's mention of the New Karner Road post office as a possible destination for Boone.

"I've got to run out on a couple of errands over lunch," she said. "You want anything?"

"A basket of clues on this Creekson file would be nice. Otherwise, nothing thanks."

"I'll see what I can do," she said before leaving.

Thinking about his own lunch, Boone decided to walk down to the Chambers, but this time, order something healthy, like a salad.

Once in the hall, he locked his door and then heard the office line ringing.

Shit! Unlocking the door, he stepped quickly up to his desk and picked up the handset.

"Boone here."

"Mr. Boone, this is Judith. Judith Hirschhorn. I need to see you."

He sighed before responding.

"When?"

"Now? Can I see you right now?"

"Where are you?"

"In my car. Outside your office."

"Okay. Come on up."

"Oh, thank you!"

He hung up the phone. Feeling his stomach rumble, he felt virtuous. Hungry, but virtuous.

Stepping out into the hall, he watched for Judith. She stepped off the elevator and, as she walked towards him, he did his best to remind himself that she that she had been used any number of ways by countless men. And on camera.

As she neared the open door, he stepped back and gestured for her to go in. She breezed past him and took a seat in one of his client chairs. He went inside, closing the door behind him. As he walked around his desk, he also closed the door between his and Marianne's office.

After taking a seat, he asked, "So, how can I help you?"

"First," she said, "I need to tell you something about myself."

She quickly twisted her head to one side, her eyes closed tightly.

He said, "If you're talking about your career in the adult film industry, I'm already aware of that. I'm not here to judge, but I'll help you if I can."

She slowly turned to look at him but did not maintain eye contact.

Saying, in a shaky voice, "You do?"

Even though she wasn't facing him, he answered her. "Yes. The internet is forever."

With her eyes squinched shut, and her head hanging, she said in a low voice, "I am so ashamed of myself."

"Again," he said, "I'm not here to judge. But before we go any further, I have something to tell you. Okay?"

"Okay, I guess."

"Nick Grimme has been here. He came to see me one day last week. While we were talking, he told me he keeps track of your, as he put it, 'comings and going.' He probably knows you're here right now."

"That doesn't surprise me."

"Even worse, he hired me to deliver a package to some customer who would pick it up on Saturday at Lafayette Park. I had no idea who the customer was. Had I known it was you, I would have refused."

"Did you see what was in the . . . "

"No. It was sealed when I received it. But you don't have to worry. I tore up his check, and I won't do any more work for him, or Hirschhorn Enterprises, if that helps."

"It doesn't, I'm afraid. I don't mean you, but . . . now, I don't know what to do."

"Tell you what," he said. "Let me get you some bottled water, give you a few minutes to think about whatever you're here to talk about, and we'll go from there. Does that work?"

She sniffed, smiled momentarily, and nodded once, but enthusiastically. "Yes. I think so."

He stood up and said, "I'll be right back. Just going down the hall for the water. Don't go anywhere."

As he walked around his desk to the door, she twisted in her seat to look at him. "I'll be right here," she said.

A few minutes later, he returned to the office. He placed a small bottle of water and a paper napkin on the desk in front of her.

"Here you go," he said. "Service with a smile."

She picked up the bottle, snapped the cap open, and took a sip.

"I may as well just tell you what prompted me to come here today."

"That would be a good place to start," he said.

"My husband is older than me. Quite a bit older actually, and he has congestive heart disease. Even the slightest bit of exertion tires him out."

Boone nodded but said anything.

She took another sip of water, then dabbed at her lips with the napkin.

"He cannot, . . . well, . . . you know. But he, uh, . . . he likes to watch me dress, and undress slowly, and I can do that for him. And sometimes," she blushed and looked away, "he likes to touch me."

"Does he know about your, um, . . . career?"

"I don't know. I'm not sure, but I don't think so."

She took a deep breath and, with a level voice, said, "Nick knows. I think he knew even before I met Entriken. And he didn't waste any time taking advantage of the situation."

"How?"

"He demanded I reenact some of my videos with him, especially the ones with bondage and blindfolds. I refused, and he said if I didn't cooperate, he would expose me to my husband."

"May I interrupt you here?" he asked.

"Sure."

"You knew it was Nick when you first came to see me, didn't you?"

"Yes," she said, her eyelids lowered. "But I thought if I told you that in the first place, you wouldn't be as interested in helping me."

"Okay. I guess I understand that. So, how did you meet Entriken? And where?"

"In Vegas. He was there at a trade show for publishers. I think most of it was beyond him. He doesn't understand technology at all. He wouldn't recognize an iPad if he sat on one."

"I wandered into the wrong reception. I didn't realize it at first, and I was looking around for someone I was supposed to meet. He walked up to me and asked me if I needed help. We had dinner the next night, and, well, it didn't take long for him to propose. His first wife had died some six months earlier, and . . . "

Flustered, she blushed, and began nervously shaking her hands in front of her until she clasped them tightly together.

"I wanted out of the biz. By then, I'd already had three abortions, and . . . he's very sweet, and very generous. I thought I was going to be okay, for maybe the first time in my life."

"But?"

"But Nick. Eventually, I agreed to have sex with him, to let him fuck me, just to shut him up. But he became more and more demanding, especially, . . I don't want to say."

"So, where are things now?"

"Hopeless. That package you dropped off for me?"

"Yes?"

"I didn't realize it, but he had some kind of camera in the room, and it's pictures of him, and me, and . . . I don't know what would happen if he showed those pictures to Entriken.

It might kill him. Maybe that's what Nick is hoping. I don't know."

"Question," he said. "Have you seen your husband's will?"

"No, but I bet Nick has. Entriken told me he's left me an allowance, but most of his property goes to this son and daughter by his first wife."

She took a small sip of water. "Oh, . . . I almost forgot. We signed a prenup before getting married. But I don't care about the money, and I don't want him to die, not that way."

"Has Nick made any other demands of you? I mean, besides sex?"

"No, but he says the sex is just for openers, or something like that. I don't know what he has in mind. I just want it to stop."

He leaned back in his chair and rested his curled fingers against his chin for a moment.

"I'm not sure there's much I can do for you. Even if we could convince Nick to stop, that won't remove what's already on the internet. There will always be another Nick out there to take advantage of you. Your best bet is to seek help from the police. Maybe legal action might also be persuasive."

"If I go to the cops, or take him to court, he'll still make sure Entriken finds out about, . . . about my past."

"Have you ever thought of just telling your husband? I don't mean showing him anything, just letting him know it's out there, and that Nick is trying to exploit you for his personal gain."

"I can't do that. Entriken has never asked me about my past, or my family, or anything."

"You tell Entriken," he said, "you take away Nick's weapons. And finally gives you peace of mind. Carrying a secret like this is a burden that only grows heavier with time."

"I can't. I just can't. Can you *do something* to Nick? You know what I mean?"

"Yeah. I know what you mean, and I'm sorry. I cannot commit a crime to solve your problems. But I *can* recommend a lawyer that is hell on wheels. If anyone can get Nick's attention, this guy will. He fights the FBI to a standstill for lunch! I'm sure he can handle Nick."

She lowered her eyes and looked at him with a smile he knew had been practiced and rehearsed for the camera countless times. Leaning forward to afford him a partial view of her breasts through her low-cut blouse, she said softly, "Is there nothing I can do to change your mind? To take care of Nick for me, once and for all?"

Feeling indescribably sad, he closed his eyes and slowly shook his head from side to side before saying, "I liked you better when you said you wanted out of the biz and told me you were ashamed of your past."

Her smile vanished; her eyes became flat as glass. She bent down to pick up her purse. Standing up and glaring at him, she said, "Go to hell."

Boone shrugged and said, "You and Nick deserve each other."

He swiveled his chair and turned his back to her. After hearing the door slam behind him, he looked out the window for a long time.

At some point, Marianne came into his office. "So, Judith left," she said. "What did she want?"

"She told me to go to hell."

"Oh. Don't you just hate that?"

"It's not the first time. But right now, lunch sounds better than hell."

TWELVE

WEDNESDAY AFTERNOON, BOONE TOOK a call from Elaine Russell. As a physician's assistant at Ellis Hospital in Schenectady, she was on an evening shift. Did he have time to see her? He did.

She arrived at half-past two, wearing scrubs under a light jacket. Boone had left the door between the two offices open. Once Elaine was settled, he asked if his assistant Marianne could sit in on the conversation. Elaine looked nervously towards Marianne's office before answering.

"I suppose so," she said. "May I ask why?"

"Marianne is my assistant," he said. "At times, I may need to involve her in an ongoing file when I can't be two places at once. She also does most of our online and public records searching. It's helpful to me if she has basic familiarity with the case."

"Okay then," Elaine said.

In a slightly louder voice, he said, "Marianne, would you like to join us?"

"Be right in, Mr. Boone," she replied.

Marianne took the other client chair, with a six by nine steno pad and pen in hand.

"Ms. Russell, can you tell us what kind of girl Geraldine was? I've spoken with a number of her classmates and friends and have a pretty good picture of her as an intelligent, focused young lady. But I think a parent's perspective is always the best gauge."

Elaine took in a deep breath and let it out. "You're not far off the mark," she said. "Geraldine was a serious student, and true to her faith." She glanced away nervously before adding, "We're Lutherans."

"Do you attend Bethlehem Lutheran?" Marianne asked.

Turning slightly to face Marianne, Elaine brightened and said, "Yes. Do you know it?"

"No," she said, "but I know of it."

Elaine smiled. "Gerry is, . . . was, I'm sorry, very active with the church's youth group in Delmar. And, of course, the three of us always attended worship on Sundays."

Wistfully, she said, "Russell and I still go, but . . . " Pulling a small hanky out of her sleeve, she dabbed at her eyes. "I'm sorry. It's just hard to understand why this had to happen to her. She was so smart."

Looking at Boone, her eyes tearing up, she said, "She wanted to become a psychologist." Then, with a chuckle, she added, "That was when she didn't want to be a large animal vet. I don't know for sure which path she would have taken, but she'd have been in the top of her field."

"Did your daughter have any boyfriends?"

"Not really, no. I mean she went on activities with the youth group, and sometimes go to a movie or meet a boy from school for some school project. I wouldn't call them dates exactly."

"Did you ever see any indication that she was experimenting with drugs?"

"Oh no," she answered. "I had long discussions with her about what I've seen at work with drug overdoses and such. I think she would never have knowingly taken anything, . . . that, . . . that night. That's why we were so surprised when they told us she had overdosed."

Looking briefly at Marianne, Boone noticed she was busy taking notes.

"I hesitate to ask this, but do you know if Geraldine was sexually active?"

Blushing slightly, Elaine answered, "No. At least I don't think so. We had, . . . you know, 'the talk' that every mother has with her daughter. And occasionally, she would come to me with questions. I was always frank, and honest with her. I like to believe she would have been a virgin on her wedding day. But, these days, . . . " she gestured helplessly, "who knows?"

"One of her friends told me Gerry was interested in developing a relationship with the boy, David Creekson. Did she ever mention anything about him to you?"

"No. But I wish she had. We didn't even know she was going to be seeing him until she asked her father to drop her off at their home. We were assured his parents were going to be there, and I believe Stanley even spoke with the young man's father that evening. I didn't think we should have allowed her to go out that evening, but she seemed so excited, . . . I don't know. I never thought she was impressed by wealthy people, and maybe that wasn't it. I just don't know."

Elaine looked down at her hands, and then again dabbed at her eyes before adding, "I think the night we got that phone call about her being taken to the hospital was the worst night of my life." Now looking away from Boone and Marianne, she said, "Worse even than when I learned my first husband had died in Afghanistan."

She sighed and shook her head.

Marianne asked, "Ms. Russell, did Geraldine have an allowance?"

Startled, Elaine turned quickly to look at her before answering. "No, she did not. But we did give her spending money whenever she needed any, and she always had what I called 'get home money' in her purse. It was fifty dollars. We, that is my husband and I, were talking about giving her an allowance at the end of the school year."

Boone then asked, "How is your husband doing?"

"He's devastated. Couldn't you see that when you came to the house?"

"I'm sorry," he said. "I don't mean to cause you distress, I was just, . . . "

"No, and I didn't mean to snap at you. I'm sorry. It's just, . . . well, you see, Stanley is sterile. It's unlikely we can ever have children. He couldn't have loved Geraldine more if she were his own daughter."

Boone nodded as Marianne continued writing.

"And you'll do whatever you can to clear her name?" Elaine asked.

"Absolutely. I won't stop until we know the truth," he assured her.

"Good." She then asked, "Is there any more you need to know? I have some errands to run before I have to go to work."

Boone looked at Marianne. "Do you have any other questions?"

"No," she said, closing her steno pad.

"I think we're done, at least for now," he said to Elaine. "If I have any other questions, may I call you?"

"Sure," she said. After giving Marianne her cell phone number, she dabbed her eyes with her hanky and returned it to her sleeve. Glancing at her watch, she said, "I really must be going now."

"Marianne will walk you out," he replied. "Thank you so much for coming in to see us."

She nodded and stood up. Marianne joined her and escorted her out of Boone's office.

When Marianne returned, he asked her, "Well? What did you think?"

"Not sure. I suspect Geraldine may have been impressed by the Creekson wealth, based on what her friends told you, that she would do anything to be the Creekson boy's girlfriend. But if so, she did a pretty good job of hiding it from her mother."

"I agree," he said. "That was a very good question you brought up about the allowance. I think you caught her off guard."

"Thanks."

"Not that I think she was trying to be deceptive," he said. "I feel for both of them, especially knowing they can't have children."

"I'll add my notes to the digital file, okay?"

"Sure," he said. "And when you're done, can you see what you can find out about Nicholas Grimme?"

She rolled her eyes. "The excitement never stops."

Boone opened his top right-hand drawer and took out his shoulder rig and handgun. He stood up to put it on, saying, "I'm going out for a bit. You're in charge."

"Where are you going?"

"Out."

"To do what?"

"Surveillance."

"Ooooh! And who are you gonna surveil?"

"I'm not sure," he said, preferring not to mention Creekson.

"Sounds mysterious."

"That's me," he said, grabbing a lightweight shell to cover his shoulder rig. "A man of mystery."

As he went out the door, he said over his shoulder, "See you tomorrow. Don't forget to lock up."

It was coming up on four o'clock by the time Boone found the perfect spot under a tree on Corporate Woods Drive and parked his Crown Vic. He had driven past the spot several times while cruising the area for vantage points. From there, he could easily watch cars exiting the underground parking garage of the building housing the offices of Cruickshank Developers. Being on the side of the street opposite the garage exit, he would be less obvious to someone leaving the area.

Spotting a Mercedes-Maybach S Class sporting the tag DVLPR from his position would be a child's play. He knew his target was in the office, having dialed the main number on his burner phone, only to be advised Mr. Creekson was 'on his line.'

Despite the shade offered by the tree, it was little time before it started warming up inside his car. He lowered both front seat windows for some cross ventilation and settled in for what could be several hours of patient observing. On the passenger seat within easy reach, he had a compact camera with digital zoom, a monocular for closer examination, and his notepad.

In a small cooler in the passenger footwell, he had a supply of bottled water and snacks. Having years of experience on stakeouts, he knew to hold off on the water for a good hour or so, because once he opened a bottle of water, he would have to drink the entire bottle in short order, so he had a makeshift urinal at the ready.

At quarter past five, he saw the gate arm at the exit swing up and a Mercedes-Maybach nose out to the concrete apron. Boone started his car, and as soon as he spotted the DVLPR tag, he put the Crown Vic in drive, letting two cars get between him and his target before pulling into traffic.

The Maybach turned right onto Albany Shaker Road, then right again on Northern Boulevard, which didn't surprise Boone. But the right turn onto New York Route 5 seemed out of the way for the direct route to the Creekson home. Everything became clear when the Maybach turned into the parking lot for the Waterworks Pub on Central Avenue.

He had to hand it to Creekson. Finding a gay bar for a drink and socializing or whatever after work less than twenty minutes from home was convenient. Wondering how long Creekson might be, he decided to open a bottle of water and have an organic beef jerky stick with a protein bar for dessert.

By seven-thirty, the Maybach not having moved, Boone figured Abe was in for the evening. Starting his car, he knew he could make it to his apartment in Latham before having to reach for the empty water bottle.

As he drove, he could not help but think of Marilyn Creekson, alone in the family mansion and grieving her dead son.

THIRTEEN

Thursday morning, Boone called Townsend.

"What do you want," Townsend growled.

"Is that any way to speak to your ever diligent and loyal sleuth?"

"Humph!"

"Okay, you got me. I need a referral."

"What kind?"

"A psychiatrist or whatever, who specializes in sexual disorders."

"I knew it was only a matter of time before you came out of the closet."

Boone was silent for a minute.

"Okay. Just kidding," Townsend said. "This have anything to do with Creekson? I remember your telling me the kid was a drug user. GHB was it?"

"Yes. Not sure we touched on this at our last briefing, but a young lady with experience, experience with him I mean, told me he liked to be under the influence of it during sex. His dealer told me pretty much the same thing. Said David liked to be 'under the nod' for sex. Somehow, I think this will help me understand better what happened the night he died. Know anyone?"

"Let me call you back," Townsend replied.

"Whenever you can."

After hanging up, Boone looked up to see Marianne standing in front of his desk.

"What?" he asked.

"Grimme. You had me research him, remember?"

"Yeah. Anything interesting?"

"I think so."

She sat down and glanced at a sheet of paper in one hand.

"When I want to find out about someone, the first thing I look at is financials, and I do as deep a dive into that as I can. It will not only tell me a lot about the person, but also suggest other lines of inquiry."

"Okay. So, what did you find?"

"He's being paid about two hundred thousand a year through Hirschhorn Enterprises. He has no other source of legal income I can find. Yet he is depositing another one fifty to two hundred a year overseas. He has accounts in Grand Cayman, Panama City and Zurich. I can't tell how much is in Zurich, the Swiss are pretty tight. But he has several millions between Grand Cayman and Panama City."

"Wow. So, what does that tell you?"

"Not sure without seeing Hirschhorn's books, but I'm willing to bet he's embezzling somehow."

"Any criminal history to support your theory?"

"He's had fraud and theft by deception convictions in New York courts. I can't get into the federal data bases so easily, so yeah."

"Okay. Keep at it. When you're done with his financials, flesh out the rest, but don't waste too much time on it."

"I thought you were done with Judith and the Hirschhorn mess."

"I am. But I'm also curious. And once I get into a case, even if the client dumps me, I still like to see things turn out for the better."

"Really?"

"Yeah. My ex used to always accuse me of having some kind of white knight syndrome."

"Well, in the Hirschhorn file, I'm thinking Don Quixote makes more sense."

"Grimme. Remember?"

"I'm on it!" She stood up and returned to her side of the office.

Later that afternoon, Townsend called Boone.

"I got someone for you, I think."

"Ready to copy," Boone replied, picking up his pen to take down the information.

"This woman's name is Deborah Pussmaid. She's a psychotherapist at the Whole Life Center on Trillium Lane.

"Where's that?"

"It's a dead-end off of Schoolhouse in Westmere. I've dealt with her in the past. She's expecting to hear from you. Okay?"

"Yeah, I guess so. What kind of name is Pussmaid, anyway?"

"British," he said. "I looked it up. Means 'young girl,' I think."

"Okay. Thanks, as always."

"Yeah." He hung up.

Boone looked at his legal pad. *Shit! He forgot to give me a phone number.* Finding the group online was quick work. Deborah Pussmaid was one of seven mental health professionals working at the center. He picked up his handset and, clicking on the link under her name, dialed Pussmaid's direct line.

"This is Deborah."

Boone was struck by the woman's even, yet comforting, tone of voice.

"Yes. Ms. Pussmaid, I was given your number by Clive Townsend, . . ."

Interrupting him, she said, "Is this Carl Boone? The detective?" now sounding much livelier.

"One and the same."

"Oh goody! I've never spoken with a real live private eye before. How can I help you?"

"I'm working a case that involves a young man who died under unusual circumstances. His sexual habits, or fixation, whatever you want to call it, suggests it may have some bearing on his murder. I'm hoping a mental health professional might help me develop some insights to better understand him."

"Interesting, but I'm afraid I can't help you."

"Oh."

"I couldn't possibly give you such an insight, as you suggest, without having met with the subject. Anything I had to say would be no more than guesswork."

"But an informed guess, couldn't you say?"

"Eh, . . . flattery is nice, but not persuasive in this case, I'm afraid."

"There are some unusual family dynamics at play here, that might help you narrow your focus somewhat. Are you sure I can't convince you? I'll buy you lunch."

"Oh my!" She laughed. "You are desperate, aren't you?"

"Well, anxious anyway."

"As long us lunch is involved, I can see you for a half hour or so before lunch on Saturday. Say eleven-thirty?"

"I don't want to mess up your weekend," he said. "You sure that's a good time for you?"

"I have morning appointments. Some of my clients work."

"Okay," he said. "I'll see you then, and thanks."

"You're welcome, I'm sure."

After hanging up, he again looked at her photograph on the center's website. Blonde shoulder length hair, broad open smile with laugh lines framing her eyes, he guessed her to be around his age.

The writeup under her photo said she helped patients examine patterns of behavior and communication unhelpful in coping or succeeding in daily living. He was interested to read she had experience with a crisis intervention team in Boston dealing with sexual abuse and trauma. He entered the appointment on his calendar, and then searched restaurants in Westmere.

Checking the time, he saw it was coming up on four-thirty. He put on his shoulder rig and covered it with a light windbreaker. Opening the door to Marianne's side of the office, he said, "I'm leaving for the day."

"Gym?"

"Nope, at least not yet. I want to take another look at Abe Creekson."

"When am I going to get to do some surveillance?"

"Not today," he said, thinking, *And not ever if I can help it.* "I'll lock up my door to the office. See you tomorrow."

"It's Friday tomorrow," she said. "Want me to bring in some donuts?"

Patting his stomach, he said, "Nope. Gotta pass on donuts."

"Bruegger's bagels?"

He looked up briefly as he thought. "Okay. Onion for me. And only one. I think there's some diet cream cheese in the kitchen."

As an afterthought, he added, "Take some money out of petty cash."

"Will do."

As he drove to his usual spot on Corporate Woods Drive, he tried to remember how much money was actually in the office's petty cash box but kept coming up with a blank.

By five, he was parked under his tree. Deciding to try some close-in reconnoitering, he got out of his car and walked across the street and through the main entrance. Keeping his ball cap and sunglasses on, and not looking directly at the security guard, a large, no-nonsense looking black man stationed behind an equally large counter, Boone scanned the building directory.

Just as he had spotted the floor, or floors as it turned out, for the Creekson empire, he saw the man he thought of as Boise coming in the front door in his peripheral vision. He slowly turned his head further away hoping not to be recognized.

Hearing retreating footsteps, he breathed a sigh of relief. Behind him, he heard the man say, "Hiya, Roscoe. How are things?"

"Good, Joey. And thank God tomorrow's Friday. Watcha doin' this weekend?"

"Boss is about to tell me, I think."

"Well, good luck then."

"Thanks."

As Boise's footsteps continued down the hall, Boone waited a moment for the sound of an elevator arriving. Just as he heard a *ding!* he pulled his iPhone out of his pocket. Pretending to be taking a call, he slowly walked out of the building.

Back in his Crown Vic, he breathed a sigh of relief. Not running into Boise, outside, or worse, on his way out of the building, was a stroke of incredible luck. Still, he wondered what the man's weekend assignment might consist of.

As it turned out, Boone spotted Boise leaving the building twenty minutes later, wearing the porkpie hat, untucked shirt, shorts, and jeans. With his monocular, Boone thought he could just make out the suggestion of a carry piece under the shirt.

Creekson's Maybach exited the underground parking garage shortly after. He drove straight home, with no detours or stops along the way. Normally, Boone would have been disappointed, considering the afternoon's surveillance a bust. But given his close call with Boise, he was relieved. If only he had a last name, Marianne could have fun creeping the man.

Having time on his hands, Boone hit the gym on his way home.

FOURTEEN

SATURDAY MORNING, BOONE STOPPED at the office before his appointment with Deborah Pussmaid. He wanted to take his paper file along with him in case he needed to refer to it during his meeting with her.

Traffic was the usual Saturday morning crush, especially around the Crossgates Mall, but he made good time, arriving at his destination ten minutes early.

Situated at the end of a cul-de-sac, the Whole Life Center looked like a converted brick ranch home surrounded by oak and maple trees still in early spring leaf. The building itself was painted white brick, with dark gray shutters and roofing. A number of cars were parked nose-in on both sides of the street.

He backed into a space opposite a a Volvo SUV. The dirt was so caked on Volvo, it was hard to tell if the vehicle was blue, or some shade of dark gray. Some wag had used a finger to inscribe 'Wash Me Please!' in the dirt caked on the back window.

Figuring the owner of the Volvo was a patient, he put down his front windows for air and waited. Shortly after eleven thirty, an older woman came out of the center, clutching her large purse close to her chest. She looked around anxiously before fixating on Boone sitting in his Crown Vic. With its different colored panels, she must have considered it threatening. She darted to her car, started it up and drove off at speed.

He got out of his car and began walking to the center. As he reached the street edge of the front walk, the front door opened, and from her online photo, he recognized Deborah Pussmaid coming to greet him. She wore a royal blue high-collared dress with three-quarter length sleeves. It draped nicely on her figure. A striking woman.

With his right hand outstretched, he said, "Ms. Pussmaid?"

"Yes. And you must be Mister Boone," she said with a smile as she shook his hand. "Clive has told me a lot about you."

"He lies all the time," he said, remarking to himself what a firm grip she had.

She laughed. "I don't think so. It's a pleasure to meet you. Come on in."

He followed her inside and into an office with her name on the door.

"Where would you like to sit?" she asked, still standing.

In front of her desk were two comfortable armchairs. A long couch graced the far wall, and a small round table with a Waterford lamp was tucked into the corner between the couch and the wall. A tall, arched window graced the far wall.

"I suppose the couch is for your patients?" he said.

"Not necessarily, although some like to use it."

"Just curious. One of these chairs is fine, thanks." He walked over to one and sat down.

She moved the other chair slightly to face him and sat down. With her legs crossed, and a note pad in one hand, she said, "Before we begin, I ask you not to mention any names, or other identifying information. I'm going to look at this as a hypothetical. Okay?"

"Of course," he said. "I understand."

"Good. Then tell me about your case."

He reached over to set his file on a corner of her desk. "To be honest, I'm not sure where to begin."

"Why not at the beginning? Do you know anything about this young man's life story?"

"Only what my researcher was able to discover, and what I learned during a fairly lengthy conversation with his mother."

"What about the father?"

"He's not someone who will talk to me."

"Why not?"

"I am working for the family of a young woman who was the suspect in his son's death. From what his wife tells me, he would use that appearance of a conflict of interest as an excuse to avoid speaking with me."

Deborah made some notes, then looked at him. "So, tell me what you know about him. The victim, that is."

"To start with, another man was his father, but not of record."

"Oh. And I suppose the mother shared that information with you?"

He nodded. "She did. But she isn't sure her husband is aware of it. According to her, her son was a very sensitive child in his early years, and apparently quite attached to her. Once the boy was, oh, I'm guessing six or seven years old, the father used to take him out frequently."

"Where?"

"The mother didn't know, but assumed to her husband's office on weekends, or to games, or movies. She did say at times they would be out so late, she would be concerned."

She made a few notes.

"I have a question."

"Yes?"

"I don't mind you taking notes, but if this is nothing more than a hypothetical, why would you do that?"

"Does it bother you that I'm making notes?"

"No."

"Well," she said, "I will be thinking about this story after you leave. And if something occurs to me, I'd like to give you a call."

"Makes sense," he said. "And I'm glad to know you would make the effort. I need all the help I can get to make sense of this case."

"Good. We agree then. Go on."

Boone took a deep breath and sat back in his chair before speaking. "As the boy grew up, he began pulling away from his father, resisting at times the idea of going out with him, but usually relenting."

"Just as a frame of reference, how old was this boy when this pulling away from his father started?"

"Sorry. I didn't ask that specific question of his mother, but I'm guessing fifteen or sixteen. He was eighteen when he died."

"Did the mother talk at all about her husband during your conversation?"

"Not much. Aside from the fact he spends a lot of time working at his office and in his home office, he hardly speaks to her. She also said he has no interest in her, before or after the son died. They sleep in separate bedrooms."

"Go on."

"Some of what I'm about to tell you, I've learned from a young woman who interacted with the son, from a drug dealer, and from surveillance conducted by my office. I've brought my file with me in case you have questions about any of it."

"Okay."

"First, the son has an unusual sexual practice. He likes to take gamma-hydroxy butyrate, GHB, . . ."

"I'm familiar with it," she said.

"Before sex."

Her eyes widened. "Really? It's usually the other way around. The man will give it to his partner, usually without telling her. It's commonly used as a date-rape drug."

He nodded. "Yes. Really. According to his dealer, and a teen-aged young woman who personally experienced this with him, he liked to be under the influence of the drug, or as his dealer put it, 'on the nod.' Then, the boy wanted his partner to do whatever she wanted with his body. I don't understand this, I mean in terms of his being able to achieve an erection, or, well, . . . to participate."

"Men can have erections with GHB," she said. "It's mostly used by homosexuals for heightened sexual experience while feeling extreme euphoria or drowsiness. They frequently use it in combination with Viagra, which is an especially dangerous mixture. Did the dealer or the young lady tell you anything else about this practice?"

"The dealer said it was like the boy wanted to have sex, but not be there for it, or not be involved with it. The girl said she felt the whole thing to be disgusting, and after putting her clothes on, left the room." He chuckled. "She said, or actually she intended to say I think, that the boy might as well have been a dildo."

Pussmaid made a few additional notes. "Interesting." Then, "I'm sorry. Did you want some water, or coffee? I should have asked."

"A small glass of water?"

She got up from her chair, placed her pad and pen on her desk, and walked over to a small refrigerator against the far wall. As she squatted down to open the door, he did his best to look as if he wasn't looking at her and admiring what he saw. She pulled out two small plastic bottles of water and sat them on top of the unit. She returned to her chair, handing one of the bottles to him.

"Here you go."

"Thanks." He snapped open the cap on his bottle and took a long drink.

"Anything else?" she asked.

"Yes. I almost forgot to mention this. According to the mother, the boy had no steady or ongoing relationship with any girl, just one or two dates at the most."

"That's not surprising."

"Why not?"

"Most young women with normal sexual urges would find such a practice emotionally unsettling."

He nodded, glancing at her note pad and pen still lying on the desk, and suspected she was thinking the discussion was nearing an end.

"So, what do you think?" he asked.

"I'm not sure," she said. "Of course, without being able to talk with the young man, this is all speculation. But this paraphilia, . . . "

"Could you explain that please?"

"Certainly. Paraphilia is a condition characterized by abnormal sexual desires, usually involving extreme or dangerous activity."

He nodded.

"As I was about to say, this sounds to me almost like someone who has been subjected to long term sexual abuse by an older man. Having gone through puberty, he wants to explore or experience heterosexual sex, but wants to limit his personal involvement in the act. I really think he could have been helped."

"Hmm," he said. "I don't know if this is at all relevant, but I believe the father to be a homosexual. He frequents a gay bar, sometimes as often as weekly, and will drop hundreds of dollars each time he goes there."

"And you say the boy is not his son, and the father has little to no interaction with his wife?"

"Yes."

"It's impossible to know at this juncture. But I'm thinking this sounds like the father, or someone else, might have been grooming the son as a homosexual throughout the boy's childhood. That would fit with what we know now. As the boy began, at least subconsciously, to realize and understand his attraction to women, of course he would begin to pull away from the father and try to explore sex with a female in some fashion. But again, without more information about the father and his personal history, all of this is speculation on my part."

He picked up his file, saying, "It might be speculation on your part, but so far, this is the only theory on this case that makes any sense. But it's still just circumstantial."

"I'm sorry, but that's the best I can do without actually seeing the boy, or his father."

"I understand."

"So, where are we going to lunch?"

"How about the Provence at the Stuyvesant Plaza? It's close and very nice, . . ."

"Great!" she exclaimed. "That is one of my favorite places." She stood, smoothed out the few wrinkles in the lap of her dress, and asked, "So, who's driving?"

"Maybe you want to look at my car first," he suggested.

They walked through the center and back outside. He pointed out his Crown Vic.

"Oh my," she said as she looked through a window at the interior. "I guess you don't have to worry about someone stealing it."

"That's why it looks the way it does. There's no radio, no CD player, nothing to attract attention. But the engine and transmission are rebuilt to factory specs, the shocks are heavy duty, and the tires are run flats. Sometimes I have to drive and park in some rough neighborhoods, so this doesn't attract any attention."

She looked at him, smiled and said, "How about I meet you there?"

"Okay."

He waited for her to walk to the far end of the parked cars, and get into hers, a BMW three series. After she started her car, he started his beast. Driving over Schoolhouse Road, a gray Nissan followed him.

FIFTEEN

"So, tell me about yourself," she said. The two of them were seated in Provence and sipping iced tea while they waited for their lunch orders.

"Not much to tell," he said. "I spent some time in the Navy and went into law enforcement when I got out. I've been there ever since."

"Clive tells me you were a state trooper."

"At first, yes. Eventually I got my bump to detective."

"How long did that take?"

"Let's see." He drummed his fingers lightly on the table as he thought. "Ten years or so, I think."

"How long were you with the state police?"

"Twenty-eight years until I retired."

"Why twenty-eight? Wouldn't thirty years have made a difference in your retirement?"

"Probably. But I was tired of the bureaucracy, the regulations, and the way the New York legislature, in their wisdom, keep making it harder to arrest and jail criminals."

"Are you married?"

He looked at her, and she colored slightly.

"I'm sorry," she said. "I don't mean to be nosy. It's just the nature of my profession, I guess. And you seem like a very interesting gentleman."

"Gentleman! Ha! That's the first time anyone has ever accused me of being one of those."

As the waitress brought their lunch salads to the table, Deborah unfolded her napkin and placed it on her lap. He followed suit.

"To answer your last question, no. I'm not married. I've been divorced almost seven years now. We have a son, just turned nineteen. They live in Rochester. I don't see him much. We used to be close, my boy and me, but lately, not so much."

"Why is that you think?"

"My ex. When he was younger, he wanted to be a policeman, which drove her crazy. The job is why we split. I suspect she's been working on him ever since. On the few occasions when we speak, I feel like I'm walking through a minefield. If I say anything critical of left-wing issues, I get this rage-filled response from him. And, well, . . . he's still just a kid. I hope he comes around one day."

He took a few bites of his salad, while Deborah nibbled on a dinner roll.

"What about you?" he asked.

"What about me?"

"Are you married?"

"No. I'm divorced as well. My former husband had a problem I couldn't help him with."

"Any children?"

"Yes. Our son is twenty-two. He's graduating from Case Western next month and going into the Navy's nuclear program. I'm quite proud of him."

"As you should be," he said. "When does Ensign Pussmaid receive his commission?"

She laughed. "Pussmaid is my maiden name I went back to it after the divorce. Alistair Clegg is his name. And the commissioning ceremony is immediately after graduation."

"Please give my congratulations to Ensign Clegg," he said.

He sipped his iced tea while she speared a small piece of romaine lettuce and a cherry tomato and ate it.

After chewing and swallowing her bite, she asked him, "Do you like being a private investigator?"

"Yes. I like the freedom of being able to work a case without defense attorneys and courts always looking over my shoulder, trying to second guess everything I'm doing."

"But you don't do anything illegal, do you?"

He hesitated before answering. "No."

"You sound as if you aren't sure."

"Well, sometimes I have to do things some might quibble with, but my license is important to me. I won't jeopardize it, no matter what the client tells me."

"And I'm betting being single works better for you with your career preference. Am I right?"

"Yes. And no. My first marriage, we were just kids, didn't last very long. And you're right. The job was what killed my second marriage. I don't think I'm marriage material anyway."

"Why not? You're still a relatively young man."

"I'm fifty-two, for what that's worth. But no. Although I very much like women in general, I don't seem to be very good at relationships, at least with them."

"*Them?* You make us sound like, I don't know, . . . aliens."

He smiled. "As ham-handed as I am around women, you might as well be."

After finishing less than half of her salad, she picked up her napkin, dabbed her lips with it, folded it carefully and placed it on the table. "I've had enough, I think."

"Me too," he said. "Ready?"

Turning her head slightly and looking at him from the corners of her eyes, she smiled and said, "I'm forty-eight, and still single." Then, looking squarely at him, continued. "I would like the occasional dinner out with someone who doesn't think he's God's gift to the universe."

He blushed and said, "Then, I'm your man. Occasionally, that is."

"Good then," she said, beginning to push her chair back.

He stood quickly and moved to assist her.

"Thanks. I can manage," she said before standing.

They walked outside and stood on the sidewalk in front of the restaurant. She turned, extended her hand, and said, "It's been nice to meet you."

He gripped her hand and said, "Likewise."

Holding onto his hand, she said softly, "I'm expecting to hear from you again." Squeezing his hand slightly before releasing it, she added, "Socially."

"Count on it," he replied.

As he drove back to his apartment, he wondered if the next weekend would be too soon to call. He was glad he took the time to wear a sports coat and tie with nice gabardine slacks for his appointment with her.

He resolved to tighten up on his diet, adopt a more regular gym schedule, and dress better. Excited at this new development in his life, he paid no attention to the gray Nissan with the broken front turn signal lens following him from several cars back.

SIXTEEN

THE FOLLOWING MORNING, MARIANNE presented Boone with her completed research into Nicholas Grimme. Through diligent work over the weekend, she was able to develop enough evidence to link the deposits into Grimme's foreign bank accounts with expenditures from Hirschhorn Enterprises, expenditures which she believed would turn out to be fraudulent.

Although his LinkedIn profile claimed an MBA from Penn State, she was also able to determine he had, at best, a GED during a work release program after a stint in the Rensselear County Jail after eighteen months for fraud.

After they had discussed her findings, she asked him, "How was your weekend? Did you meet with that psychiatrist?"

"I did," he said, "and it was very interesting, in more ways than one."

"Oh?" She arched her eyebrows. "Tell!"

"There may be a social opportunity for me. Have to see. But at least it was helpful on the file."

"Will it open up the case?"

"No, I don't think so. She had a good theory from the available facts, but it's all pretty circumstantial."

He told her about Pussmaid's suggestion the Creekson boy may have been the victim of sexual abuse during his childhood by the father.

"But," he added, "without more information about the father's personal life, and his life choices, we may have reached the end of the road."

"I am sorry to hear that," she said. "If Abe Creekson has anything else going on over the internet, he's doing it under some other persona, because there's nothing out there that seems to tie into him, and whatever he's doing outside of work."

Boone sighed and gathered her printed sheets into a neat stack and, holding them upright between both hands, tapped the bottom edges on his desktop to even the pages out.

"You already have all this in digital form, right?" he asked.

"Of course," she said. "Where do you think the printout came from?"

"Sorry," he said. "I've got a lot on my mind lately."

"You're forgiven," she said.

"Well, since you're in such a forgiving mood, have you had a chance to start on our month-end financials? It is the last day of the month."

"Yes," she said, "as boring as they are. Our operating account is down a bit. You have a number of hours in the Creekson file. The time on the other files isn't that great. Want me to send Clive a bill?"

"I'd rather have a result to share with him before I bill it."

"Okay. Our operating account is down, *a lot*. I recommend we bill Clive so we can catch our breath."

"Really?" he asked.

"Well, you've been spending a lot of time on Creekson, and on Hirschhorn. And we don't even have a paying client on Hirschhorn."

"Okay," he said. "Bill Clive. I'll give him a call later in the week to bring him up to date."

"I'm on it," she said, returning to her office.

Hell of a way to start off the week, he thought as he listened to the clickety-clack of her keyboard.

As she typed, he took a few minutes to type up his own notes to summarize his conversation with Pussmaid for the file.

When finished with that, he picked up the printouts on Grimme and read through them again. After finishing with them, he got up, put on his shoulder rig, and slipped on a sports jacket to cover it.

"I'm heading out."

"Where you going?" she asked.

"To talk to Grimme."

"Why?"

"To sort this mess out once and for all."

"I thought you were done trying to help Judith," she said.

"I'm not trying to help Judith," he replied.

"Well then who exactly are you trying to help?"

"Her husband."

"What? Why?"

"I have no damned idea," he said, slamming the door behind him as he left.

Half an hour later found him parking on New Courtland Street in Cohoes outside the low one and a half story building housing Hirschhorn Enterprises. Although from the outside it appeared to be a run of the mill industrial structure of some sort, looks were deceiving. Going through the front entrance, Boone found himself standing in a very upscale reception area.

Sitting behind a large workstation fashioned from teak with a granite countertop sat two attractive young ladies, both wearing boom mic headsets and handling calls of some nature. A third woman, older but smartly dressed, sat between them.

"May I help you sir?" she asked.

He walked up to the counter and handed her one of his business cards. "I'd like to speak with Mr. Grimme."

"Oh," she said. "I'm not sure that will be possible. He's quite a busy man."

"Tell him it involves the Grand Cayman account, and that I'll wait as long as it takes for him to see me."

"Yes sir," she said, nodding once as she picked up a handset.

Boone walked over to a seating area and made himself comfortable. Hirschhorn Enterprises seemed a very busy place. Younger, sharply dressed women on stiletto heels flitted through the reception area, obviously on errands of serious importance. He wondered if any of them were 'models' in the company's 'adult' publications, or porn stars writhing on camera.

Twenty minutes after talking his seat, Nick Grimme came out to greet him.

"Mr. Boone," he said, holding out his hand. "How nice to see you again.

"Thank you for seeing me," Boone replied, ignoring Grimme's hand.

After a second, Grimme let his hand drop to his side. "Won't you come with me?"

Boone followed Grimme down a short hallway to a highly polished door with a sign on it reading 'Nicholas Grimme, Vice-President.'

Grimme entered the office first with Boone close behind.

As he walked behind his desk, Grimme gestured towards the two armchairs in front of the desk. "Have a seat," he said.

Once seated himself, Grimme said, "What do you want?"

"Just checking to see if you had any more deliveries for me," Boone said. "Or was that package for Judith a one-off?"

"You said you wanted the first delivery to be a one-off," Grimme replied. "Of course, we expected you to figure out who the delivery was for. And we know she came to see you afterwards. Can you tell me what you two discussed?"

"No."

"Why then are you here?"

"A good question, which I'm here to answer."

Grimme leaned back in his high-backed leather chair, steepled his fingertips together under his chin, grinned and said, "I'm all ears."

Leaning forward so his jacket would fall open to reveal his shoulder holster, Boone said, "I'm not going to waste much of my time, or yours. I want you, . . . no, I'm telling you to leave Judith and her husband alone. And to stop stealing from the company."

"Stealing? That's a pretty serious charge. Can you back it up?"

"Let's put it this way. If the State Bureau of Criminal Investigations starts looking over the books of this place, along with the banking records from Grand Cayman, Panama City and Zurich, you will have some pretty serious explanations to make."

"You honestly think any bank in those countries will comply with a subpoena from the New York Bureau of, . . . whatever you call it."

"Probably not. But once they figure out how much money is going out of here to pay fraudulent invoices, I'm sure they'll ring up the FBI's Albany field office, who will be happy to knock on the doors of these foreign banks. I can give them actual dollar amounts if it comes to that. And don't forget the IRS. I understand they love going after people like you."

"And what if I don't comply with your demands?"

"What if I insist?"

"How insisting do you think you can be?"

"Like a blowtorch. Judith's husband may be missing a step, but he won't take kindly to learn someone he's treated well is stealing from him."

"Why do you care what Entriken thinks about anything, or anybody?"

"Letting you skate on past embezzling is not the outcome I would have preferred, but if it lets this old man live out what's left of his life in peace, and brings an end to your extortion of Judith, that's enough for me."

"I don't think I'm interested in what you're selling."

"Fine. I was on the BCI for twenty some years before I retired. I still have friends there, any one of which would be drooling at the chance to get into a case like this. I'll make the call right now."

"And what's that gun you're packing supposed to be for? Is that to scare me?"

"No. Just to keep you here until the state police show up."

Boone reached into his shirt pocket and pulled out his iPhone. Looking down at it, he began looking for his contact at the New York State Police Bureau of Criminal Investigations. Hearing the sound of a desk drawer being slowly opened, he stopped.

Grimme was slowly lifting an airweight Smith and Wesson .38 caliber revolver out of his drawer when Boone said, "Put it on the desk."

Grimme looked up to see Boone training his Colt .45 on his face. He cautiously laid the small revolver on the desk.

The two sat silent for some time until Grimme broke the silence.

"Okay. Maybe I'm willing to consider what you want."

"Good. Oh. There is one more thing."

"And that is?"

"You will resign from Hirschhorn Enterprises, effective immediately, and leave the state."

Grimme snorted. "I can't do that."

"It's only a matter of will. Surely you have enough money to live very comfortably anywhere else in the world."

"You don't understand."

"Enlighten me," Boone said, his grip on the Colt not wavering.

"It's not so much the money," Grimme said. "It's the getting of it that's such a fascinating game. Someone once said sex is like money. Too much is just enough."

Shaking his head slowly, Boone said, "Games up. This is the only way to make sure you live up to your end of the deal."

Boone reached across the desk, picked up the airweight and slid it into an outer pocket of his jacket.

"Thanks for this by the way," he said, holstering his own handgun. "So. Are we in agreement?"

His eyelids closed, and his lips compressed into a thin line, Grimme did not reply immediately. Then, looking up at Boone, he said, "I don't think I have any other choice."

"Good. You can announce your resignation to all of the employees over the firm's network, can you not?"

"What? You mean *now?*"

"Right now. You can say its for personal reasons, or more time with your family, . . . "

"I don't have a family."

"I'm not surprised. How about 'to pursue other ventures?' "

"I guess that's as good a reason as any."

"Start typing."

As Grimme composed his firm-wide email, Boone walked around to the back of the desk to look over Grimme's shoulder. Grimme typed slowly, muttering to himself.

Without attempting to look up at Boone, when he was finished, he said, "This enough for you?" The message read:

Fm: nicholasg@hirschhorne.com
To: allstaff
I am announcing my resignation from Hirschhorn Enterprises LLC effective immediately to pursue other ventures.
Nicholas Grimme

"Okay," Boone said. "Send it."

After Grimme clicked on the 'send' icon, he said, "There. It's gone. You happy now?"

"Almost. If you really sent it to a valid address, responses should start showing up in your inbox."

Even as Boone spoke, Grimme's computer began repeatedly signaling incoming new mail.

"Open one," Boone said.

Grimme clicked on the first email, which came from *sharonm@hirschhorne.com*. **Sorry to see you go. This place won't be the same without you.** Her text was followed by six crying emojis.

"Good," Boone said. "My work here is finished. I'll see myself out."

SEVENTEEN

DRIVING BACK TO THE office, Boone knew Grimme would not stay in the box he was in. It might take the man weeks, or even months, but he would do his level best to find a way to renege on his commitments to walk away from Hirschhorn Enterprises and leave the state.

All his efforts had accomplished that morning was to force Grimme to be more circumspect, and much more cautious in the future. The BCI, and probably the FBI, would eventually become involved in untangling Grimme's frauds at some point. That much was a certainty.

Unlocking his door at the office, he was surprised to see the inner door separating Marianne's section from his closed. Trying to open it, he found it to be locked as well. He knocked on the door.

"Who is it?" she yelled.

"Me," he yelled back. "Who do you think?"

He could detect some rustling on the other side of the door, and the sounds of the deadbolt and lockset being unlocked.

Marianne opened the door, and said, "Just being sure, that's all. We had a visitor while you were gone."

Feeling apprehensive, he asked, "Who was it?"

"Not sure. He was a big, enormous! He didn't tell me his name or what he wanted. Just wanted me to tell you that you had been warned too many times."

"What did he look like?"

"Big!" she shouted. "I don't know, just that he scared the hell out of me. I think he had some kind of gun in his pocket."

"Was he wearing a porkpie hat?"

"Yeah. Jeans, sneaks and a dirty polo shirt."

"I know who it is. He's been here before. I think he works for Abe Creekson. He told me last time he was here to stop working the file if I didn't want to wind up behind the New Karner Road post office."

She took a step back, her face going pale as she brought her fingertips up to her chin. Her voice rising in alarm, she said, "And you didn't tell me that?'

"I didn't want you to worry. Guys like this are usually more bark than bite, and . . . "

"Yeah! Until they're not," she interrupted. "I don't like being here alone when you're gone. I know there can be dangerous people showing up here. I try to keep the place locked up, and my pepper gel close at hand when you're out."

"What did I tell you about pepper sprays and such?"

"I don't remember."

"I do, even though it's been a while. Pepper spray or mace are no good if the other person has a gun. Remember?"

"Yeah. I guess so."

"How did he get in?"

"Someone," she looked straight at him, "must have left their door unlocked when someone left earlier."

"And someone else," he replied, "didn't check the locks, I'm guessing."

"Okay, point taken. But what are we going to do?"

He reached down and patted the jacket pocket holding Grimme's airweight revolver.

"*We* are going to lunch."

"And how's that going to help office security?"

"And," he continued, "after lunch, we're going to the range."

"I don't like guns," she said. "They scare me."

"That's because you've probably never handled one. Right?"

"True. But still, they're very dangerous to have."

"Only if you don't know how to use one, or how to handle one safely."

They regarded each other. Finally, she said, "Okay, I guess."

"Get your stuff. Let's lock up and head out."

"How'd things go with Grimme?" she asked.

"I'll tell you on the way."

During the drive, Boone noticed a gray Nissan with a busted turn signal following them. Uncertain but wary, he kept his silence. A less observant person might put it down to coincidence, but he did not believe in coincidence. He tried to make out the front license plate but couldn't, given the heavy traffic.

* * *

Forty-five minutes later, he pulled into the parking lot at Frank's Diner on Lower Hudson Avenue, Green Island, New York. The gray Nissan did not slow down but continued up Lower Hudson Avenue.

The menu selections in the diner were limited, but Boone vouched for the quality of the food.

"How did you find this place?" she asked.

"It's close to the range I like to go to," he said.

"Looks like it's mostly sandwiches and subs," she said as she scanned the menu.

"I recommend their BLT on multi-grain toast. Excellent," he said.

"Well, that's a bit more than I usually have at lunch, but okay. BLT it is."

After the waitress had delivered their orders, Marianne said, "That's fast."

"Yep," he replied. "The food's good, there's plenty of it, and they don't waste your time. That's why I like this place."

After taking a bite of her sandwich, she said, "Damn! This is great!"

"Beats a yogurt for lunch, don't you think?"

"Yeah. Maybe not every day, but . . ."

"Don't forget," he said. "The multi-grain toast is good for you, as are the tomato and the lettuce."

After chewing and swallowing a bite, she grinned and said, "But the bacon? What about the bacon?"

"Someone once said their holy trinity was olive oil, salt and bacon, claiming bacon always made it, whatever *it* is, better. Do you like New England clam chowder?"

"Oh yes Especially on a snowy day in January," she admitted.

"You know what's in that?"

"Yeah, I know. Bacon. But . . . "

"No buts about it. Bacon and pork products are a must in my diet. Do you know who Kat Timpf is?"

"No."

"She's a conservative columnist, but also pretty funny in her own right."

"Okay."

"She said that there is absolutely no reason why bacon flavored envelope glue should exist, let alone be so popular that it's always sold out."

Marianne laughed. "Okay. Bacon rules. In your house anyway. Let me finish this scrumptious sandwich."

He nodded and continued to work on his own lunch.

Despite her appreciation for the sandwich, Marianne could barely finish half of hers. "Can I get the rest of this to go?" she asked.

"Absolutely," he told her. "But it may not be as good later. Give it a shot."

"No pun intended?"

"Not at all." He motioned to the waitress and pantomimed writing a check with his hands.

When she brought the check, he asked her for a 'to-go' container while he filled out the charge slip, added a tip, and laid it with his credit card on the table.

Once outside, Boone put the 'to-go' container in his car and pointed up the street. "That's where we're going," he said. "You want to walk two blocks? Or ride?"

Looking distastefully at his car, she said, "Walking is better for you. Besides, I need to work off this huge lunch."

"This way then."

Five minutes later, they stepped inside entrance to American Tactical Systems. Walking between the various locked display cases showing dozens of different models of semi-automatic handguns and revolvers, Boone headed for the main counter.

"Carl! How ya been?" shouted the clerk behind the counter.

"Good, Jimmy. Can't complain. I got a new shooter with me today." He turned his head and nodded to indicate Marianne coming up beside him.

"Have you been here before, Miss?"

"Uh, no. No, I haven't."

"Well then, you'll need to fill out a new shooter form and then we can go over a few safety precautions, okay?"

"Okay." She stepped up to the counter as Jimmy put a two-page form down in front of her and handed her a pen.

Turning to Boone, Jimmy said, "Will she need ears and eyes?"

"Yes. But depending on how things go today, we'll be getting her some, along with a range bag. You got any thirty-eight range ammo?"

"Sure. How much?"

"A box of twenty-five ought to be more than enough for today."

"Comin' right up."

Jimmy turned around, picked up a small box of ammo, and placed it on the counter.

"Two lanes?" he asked. "Or you going to share one."

"I think sharing today, half an hour. I just want to give her the feel of handling and discharging a weapon. If she is comfortable with it, we'll get her into one of your safety classes."

"Sounds good," the clerk replied. Then, turning to Marianne, he said, "How you comin' there?"

"Okay, I guess. It says here you need to see my driver's license?"

"Please."

She rummaged through her purse for her wallet, and pulled it out, handing it to Jimmy.

He made a few notes on her form, and said, "Here's a list of basic safety precautions while on the firing station. Carl here will answer any questions you have. Why don't you read these over while I get your equipment?"

"Okay," she said, looking from side to side.

A few minutes later, Jimmy placed a pair of safety glasses and 'Mickey Mouse' hearing protectors on the counter in front of her.

"Here you go," he said. "You need to put those on before going through the door to the firing lanes."

Boone bent down and said, "Give me a second to go to my locker and pick up own gear, okay?"

"You have a locker here?" she asked.

"Yeah. But only because I became a member while I was with the state police. I couldn't do it now."

"Oh, come on Carl," Jimmy said. "We'd take care of you, you know that."

Boone nodded before going over to the far side where stood a bank of lockers with combination locks on those in use.

Returning to Marianne with his gear in hand, he said, "Ready?"

She took in a deep breath. "Ready as I'll ever be."

"Okay then. Let's put on our safety gear and go shoot!"

Jimmy said, "Lane six, Carl. It's all yours. Have fun!"

Even with the hearing protectors in place, Boone could hear the muffled sound of gunfire on the other side of the two steel doors separating the firing stations from the store side of the range. From the way her blouse fluttered below the collar, he could tell that Marianne was nervous.

* * *

After twenty minutes of test firing Grimme's little airweight under Boone's patient instruction, Marianne had learned about a relaxed shooter's stance, sight alignment, breathing, and smooth trigger pull. On her last two full cylinder firings, she was making respectable hits on the targets' center mass at twenty feet and grinning like a school kid at Disney World.

Bending low so she could hear him through her hearing protectors, he said, "Would you like to try my Colt forty-five?"

Smiling, she nodded enthusiastically.

He pulled it out of his shoulder rig, popped the magazine out and pulled the slide back to eject the round in the chamber. Showing her the unobstructed view through the handle of the gun, he said, "Verify for me the weapon is unloaded." She nodded.

"Okay then." He released the slide forward, and replaced the ejected round in the magazine. Handing her the gun with the barrel pointed down range, he told her to slide the magazine into the handle.

She took the gun and yelled, "This thing weighs a ton!"

"Yeah," he replied. "And it will stop a ton as well."

Explaining how to pull the slide back to put a round in the firing chamber, he told her to operate the slide. She eventually managed to after two tries.

"Now, remember everything I told you. Stance, alignment, firm grip on the handle, breathe, and trigger pull. You ready?"

She nodded and lined up the sights. He quickly stepped behind her. When she fired the first round, the boom echoed throughout the range and the recoil knocked her back into his waiting arms. Once she collected herself, she laid the weapon down on the bench in front of her. Turning to face him, she said, "What is that thing? A cannon?"

He smiled and nodded his head towards the target. Even from twenty feet, she could see the difference in the size of the holes left by her .38 range ammo as opposed to the gap left by the .45 hollow point. She also noted her shot missed the target's head by more than a few inches.

"You want to try it again?" he asked.

"Okay. One more," she said. "Maybe this time, I won't get knocked on my ass!"

"Remember, once you fire a round, your next one is ready to go. This is a loaded weapon."

She nodded, and again, picked up the gun, adopted her stance, lined up her sights, took in a deep breath, let it out, and slowly squeezed the trigger. Again, the sound of the discharge echoed against the concrete block walls on all sides of the range. But this time, she held her position without being bounced back by the recoil and took out the target's neck.

Laying the gun down on the bench, she turned to Boone. "I think I've had enough for today," she said.

He smiled, put the Colt back in his shoulder rig, her unused ammo and the airweight in his jacket pockets.

"Okay. We can head back to the office now."

Before leaving the range, Marianne signed up for a pistol safety course, and Boone left Grimme's airweight behind for cleaning, and to get it ready for later transfer to her.

In the car on the way back to the office, Marianne could not stop talking about how much fun she had firing the airweight, how heavy and loud the forty-five was, and how ravenously hungry she felt. She finished the rest of her BLT long before Boone reached the parking lot.

Once he could get a word in edgewise, he asked her, "How did you like that little thirty-eight?"

"Oh, it's perfect. It fits my hand, and the recoil is no problem. I liked it a lot."

"Well then," he said, "it's yours. A friend gave it to me, and one thing I don't need is another handgun. Once you've finished your safety course, we'll file the purchase permit, get you registered, and you'll be all set. Does this make you feel better?"

"Yes," she said. "Thanks. I do feel a lot better." Then, thinking about it, she added, "That is, once the gun is legally mine and I have it close at hand. But for now, I guess both of us will have to be better at keeping the place locked up."

"Agreed," he said.

EIGHTEEN

BOONE WAS SCANNING THE Thursday morning online edition of the Albany Times-Union when Detective George Tucker walked into his office. Tucker was a colleague of Boone's from their days together in the state police BCI. Boone had always considered Tucker, or Tuck as he was known, to be a straight shooter.

Surprised at seeing him, Boone said, "George! How the hell are you?" He stood up to shake his friend's hand. "It's good to see you. Want a cup of coffee?"

Tucker did not return the smile, and his handshake was perfunctory. "Sorry, Carl," he said, "but you have to come with me."

"What?"

"You have to come with me. Look, I'm trying to ask nice here, okay?"

"Where are we going?"

"Troop G, Carl. We need to interview you about a case."

"Be straight with me here, George. Am I a suspect? A wit? Or does someone just want to pick my brain?"

"I can't get into that right now, Carl. I'm sorry."

"I get it. So you, or someone, want to eliminate me as a suspect. Am I going to be cuffed?"

"No, Carl. But are you carrying?"

"Yeah."

"Can you just leave it here?"

"Sure."

Boone slipped off his baggy shirt, took off his shoulder rig, and stowed it in the top right-hand drawer of his desk, and locked the desk. After putting the baggy shirt back on, he stuck his head in Marianne's side and said, "I gotta go out for a while with this guy. Should be back in an hour or two."

"Okay," she said. "You'll lock your hall door?"

He nodded.

As he and Tucker were leaving, Boone could hear Marianne closing and locking the door between their offices. She had filed the paperwork permitting her to purchase a handgun but hadn't yet heard from the Albany County Sheriff's office. Until then, whenever Boone was out of the office, she was locked up tighter than Fort Knox. At least it felt that way to her.

As Tucker drove his unmarked D ride towards Latham, Boone was wishing he had offered to drive himself, since Troop G headquarters wasn't far from his own apartment.

He knew better than to engage Tucker in conversation during the transport. As it was, he tried to convince himself he should be grateful he wasn't in handcuffs and riding in the back, 'cuffed and stuffed,' as they called it.

Once they had arrived at Troop G, Tucker took Boone to an interview room, told him to have a seat, and left him alone. Hearing the door locked was unsettling. He tried telling himself that he was innocent of any wrongdoing, and that this had to be some sort of misunderstanding. But he remained unnerved, knowing how New York's criminal justice system more often resembled Alice's wonderland than what any reasonable person might expect.

When a perp, typically some kid doing something stupid, was being interviewed, almost invariably those from nicer homes would fall back on the lessons drilled into them from childhood on. 'Always tell the truth,' his parents would preach. 'It will be better for you if you do.'

So, the kid admits to everything, providing corroborating details. And presto! He gets charged with every conceivable count. Defense attorneys pleading for lenience, or mercy, are often met with scorn by assistant district attorneys.

"What do you mean, go easy on this kid?" they would say. "I got a confession, and you want me to ignore these charges?"

Boone waited for someone to show up and interview him. He knew the tactic. Let the suspect sweat alone for an hour or so before questioning. Not wanting to give them any edge, he avoided looking at the two-way mirror on the far wall, or the camera mounted in the far top corner of the room.

After a half hour of solitary confinement, he crossed his arms on the table and put his head down. As he suspected, at that moment, the door to the room was unlocked and thrown open. A New York State Police major Boone didn't recognize entered the room, with Detective Tucker following.

"Good morning, Mr. Boone. I am Major Dimmick. I believe you know Detective George Tucker?"

Boone nodded.

"Sorry to keep you waiting," Dimmick said. "You know how it is."

Boone bit the inside of his cheek to keep from laughing.

"Did you want anything? Coffee? Juice? Some water?"

"No thanks," Boone said. "I'm good, at least for now. Can we just get down to why I'm here? I don't want to miss lunch."

Major Dimmick pulled out a chair on the side of the table opposite Boone and sat down. Tucker stood back in the corner next to the door, his arms crossed over his chest, looking like he'd rather be anywhere else.

"Mr. Boone, do you know a Judith Hirschhorn?"

Thinking to himself, *What the hell is this all about?* he said, "Yes. Not well."

"Was she ever a client of yours?"

"No. I met with her twice. She never hired me."

"How about a Nicholas Grimme?"

Boone was surprised, not by the question but by the speed with which Grimme might be attempting to get out of his commitments. He gave no visible reaction.

"Yes. I've met with him twice."

"And what were those meetings about?"

"He came to me to discuss my professional relationship with Mrs. Hirschhorn. I told him there wasn't one. He also discussed possibly hiring me on behalf of his employer."

"That would be," the major looked down at his notes, "Hirschhorn Enterprises, correct?"

"Yes."

"And did he hire you?"

"Yes."

"Can you tell me the nature of the work he asked you to perform on behalf of his employer?"

"No."

"Why not?"

"You should know why not. But I will tell you that afterwards, I tore up his check and declined further employment with that company."

"Okay." Major Dimmick made some notes. "Moving on, did you meet with Mr. Grimme a second time?"

"Yes."

"Can you tell me what was discussed at that meeting?"

"I asked him to discontinue his attempts to blackmail Mrs. Hirschhorn."

"You asked him at the point of a gun, did you not?"

"No. Although he knew I was carrying a weapon, the only time I drew it was when he attempted to retrieve a revolver from his desk drawer."

Major Dimmick leaned into his chair, tilted his head back and, looking at Boone through half-lidded eyes, said, "Interesting. Mr. Grimme tells us you forced him to resign from the company, and that you stole a revolver from him before leaving the premises. Is there anything to that?"

"I suggested to him that his resignation might be in the best interests of Mrs. Hirschhorn and his employer, but no. He didn't *have to do* anything."

Waiting for the next question, it surprised Boone when the major didn't further explore what happened with Grimme's revolver.

"Mr. Boone, do you know an Entriken Hirschhorn?"

"No."

"Do you know of him?"

"Yes. I believe him to be the senior partner of the Hirschhorn company, but that's all."

"Would you be surprised if I were to tell you that Mr. Entriken Hirschhorn was found dead last night at his home, having been shot twice in the head at close range with a thirty-eight caliber revolver?"

"Yes," Boone replied, thinking, *Here comes the question about Grimme's gun*. "That would surprise me very much."

"Mr. Boone, do you own a thirty-eight caliber revolver?"

"No."

"Do you have in your possession, or do you have ready access to, a thirty-eight caliber revolver?"

"No," Boone replied, thinking *As long as it's with the range, I don't have it, or ready access to it.*

"Would it surprise you to learn that, according to Mrs. Hirschhorn, you murdered her husband, and having forced Nicholas Grimme to resign from the company, you wanted her to marry you so that you could take over the business?"

Boone laughed out loud. "That is the most ridiculous thing I've ever heard!"

"Mr. Boone, had you ever had sex with Mrs. Hirschhorn?"

"No," Boone said, feeling his neck flushing. "And I wouldn't fuck her with *your* dick!" he shouted. "Do you know what she is?"

"Mrs. Hirschhorn's background is not at issue here. We're simply investigating the murder of her husband, along with, . . . " he looked down at his notepad, "a few other things."

After looking at Boone for a long count, the major asked, "Where were you yesterday evening, between the hours of seven p.m. and ten p.m.?"

"In my apartment."

"Doing what?"

"Whatever I pleased. I had a drink, I made dinner, I watched some television, and retired early."

"Were you alone?"

"Meaning, can someone verify that?" Boone asked.

"Yes," Dimmick replied.

"No. But," Boone said, "the shows I watched were streamed over my WiFi network, which can be checked. And I'm quite sure that business, homeowner, and traffic cameras, not to mention the cameras at my apartment complex, can recreate my travels and whereabouts at all times before, during, and after the hours you are so worried about."

"Given your interactions with Mrs. Hirschhorn and Mr. Grimme, do you have any thoughts about this case you care to share with us?"

"Oh. So now, I'm one of the good guys?" Boone asked.

"I wouldn't go that far," Major Dimmick said.

"Well, here's what I think," Boone said, "and it's supposition. A gut feel if you want to call it that."

Major Dimmick nodded.

"I think Nicholas Grimme, who has a history of misdirection and fraud, has been embezzling from his employer. He may be stashing these funds in foreign bank accounts. He's also has, or had, some kind of intimate relationship with Mrs. Hirschhorn. That's based on information she has shared with me, so it may or may not be true. But I think he's the one you want to look at."

"What about her?"

"I can't tell you. I don't know if she's in on it with Grimme, or if he has some kind of hold on her and she feels she has no choice."

Major Dimmick closed his notepad. "Thank you for your cooperation, Mr. Boone. You should not consider yourself eliminated from our investigation at this stage, so I'd appreciate it if you didn't leave the area. Any plans to do so? A vacation? A cruise?"

"No," he said. "No plans, and no plans to make plans. Are we done here?"

"For now, yes. Detective Tucker will give you a lift back."

Major Dimmick stood up. Looking down at Boone, he said, "And we're not done talking about that thirty-eight." He left the room.

Boone remained in his chair, glaring at Tucker.

Glancing up at the mirror, Tucker said, "Come on, Carl. Let me get you back." He left the room. After a minute, Boone followed.

Once they were in Tucker's ride, Boone said, "George, what the fuck was that? Huh?"

"Carl, no one here believes you have anything to do with this. No one. Not even Major Dimwit, who thinks he's destined to be the Superintendent of the state police. But he had to go through the motions."

"You could have given me a heads up," Boone said. "I mean, I thought we go back!"

"We do Carl. And I'm sorry. I just thought it would be better if you weren't clued in so your answers, and your reactions, wouldn't look staged. You know?"

"Yeah, I guess so," Boone said, still upset.

"One thing though," Tucker said. "If you know anything about the revolver, the one Grimme says you stole? You better be real careful with that."

"I don't understand this business about that." Boone said. "Why didn't he press me on the gun?"

"I'm not supposed to tell you this, but she claims you stole the revolver used to kill her husband from Grimme. We know Grimme, if he had a gun, it would have been illegal with his felony convictions. We're checking to see if there's any gun registered under his name."

Everything became clear to Boone at that point.

"Tuck," he said, now using Tucker's nickname as a friend and colleague would, "if I gave you the serial number of a handgun, let's say hypothetically, could you look it up?"

Tucker glanced over at him, his eyebrows furrowed. "Would this hypothetical gun be a thirty-eight caliber revolver?"

"I don't know. Maybe."

"I'd need a case number, . . . Hell's bells. I can just use this case. Call me when you want to."

They rode on in silence, until Tucker said, "Man. That Judith Hirschhorn, she is one sweet looking piece of ass, isn't she?"

"Yeah, I suppose so. But you'd be the ten-thousandth guy to tap it if you did."

"Oh, I'd never do that to Mazie. She'd nut me."

Boone laughed, thinking of Tucker's wife, Mazie. "Yeah. She certainly would."

As Tucker pulled up in front of Boone's building, he reached over to shake hands. "No hard feelings?"

Boone shook his hand before getting out. "No. I guess not. Keep the faith, brother."

NINETEEN

LATE FRIDAY MORNING, BOONE worked up his courage to dial Deborah Pussmaid's direct line. As he heard the ring tone at the other end of the line, he began drumming the fingers of his free hand on the desktop. He remembered her saying she might like an occasional dinner out with him, or was it someone like him? Or someone interesting? Is it too soon to call? He couldn't remember and was on the verge of breaking off the connection when she answered.

"Detective Boone," she said. He could hear the smile in her voice. Taking in a deep breath, he let it out slowly before speaking.

"Ms. Pussmaid," he said.

"Please. Deborah, or Debbie if you prefer, is fine."

He said, "Well then, Carl works for me," thinking *So far, so good.*

"Carl, how can I help you?"

He liked the sound of his name on her voice. "This is not a business call."

"Oh. Do I have to guess?"

"Sorry," he said. "I'm making a hash out of this. I'm calling to see if you're free for dinner tomorrow evening."

He heard some muffled speech on the other end, as if she had her hand over the phone while speaking to someone in her office.

"Sorry," she said. "I'm back. I just had something to take care of."

"I can call back if you like," he said.

"No, it's fine. And yes. I'd love to have dinner with you tomorrow evening. Did you have any place in mind?"

Shit! Talk about not planning ahead!

"It's been a long time since I've gone out to dinner. I'm open to anything."

"Do you like Italian?"

"Love it," he said, grateful for any suggestion at this point.

"How about Delmonico's Steakhouse on Central Avenue in Colonie? Ever been there?"

"No," he said.

"It's one of my favorites, and you won't be disappointed."

"I look forward to it."

"What time?"

"How about I pick up at seven?" he said.

She was quiet. Was she having second thoughts?

"Please don't take this the wrong way, but how about if I meet you there?"

"I guess so," he said, wondering what brought this on. Was she nervous about riding with him? Did she not want him to know where she lived?

"It's, . . . I don't know how quite to say this, but . . . "

"It's usually best to get it out," he said, "instead of beating around the bush. If you're having second thoughts, . . . "

"Oh no," she interrupted. "It's not that at all," she said. "I don't want to seem pretentious, and I know you have to drive through some rough neighborhoods and all, . . ."

"Oh," he said, suddenly realizing what her concern was. "I'm sorry. I completely forgot. Yes, you're right. My car is not something any self-respecting person would want to be seen in. Sometimes, even I don't much want to be in it. Listen, I can rent, . . . "

"Let's stop being silly about this," she said. "You come by at, what did you say? Seven? And we'll go in your car. Or you can drive mine."

With a sense of relief, he said, "See you at seven. What's the address?"

"I'm three doors down from the center on Trillium. One Ninety-Five."

"That's convenient," he said. "See you at seven, Deborah." He couldn't bring himself to address a grown woman as 'Debbie.'

"Sure," she said. "It's a date. Let me give you my home number, in case you need to reach me."

After taking down her number and saying goodbye, he hung up the phone, feeling pleased with himself. Thinking it was time to think about life outside work, he decided to look at a second car for social occasions. Bringing up his browser, he searched area Ford-Lincoln dealerships.

Halfway through his search, Marianne came in to see him.

"Here," she said, handing him a note. "This came with Clive's check on our latest bill on Creekson."

Boone took the note. It read 'What's up? C.'

"Thanks. I'll call him after lunch."

She nodded and returned to her office.

He sat the note on his desk where he wouldn't miss it after lunch. Going back to his computer, he decided to take a run out to Fucillo Lincoln on Central Avenue during lunch.

As he walked down South Pearl to the parking lot, he felt enthusiastic. It was a perfect day in early June. The weather was pleasant, most of his files were in good shape, and best of all, he had a date for Saturday night. As he approached his car in the lot, he was wondering if it was appropriate to bring flowers to Deborah's house the next evening.

Standing next to his car, Boone reached into his pocket for his car keys when he glimpsed a large man wearing a porkpie hat on the far side of a gray Nissan next to his Crown Vic. He was holding a handgun equipped with a suppressor and aiming it at Boone.

Quickly turning his upper body to the left to reduce his target profile, Boone reached for the Colt on his left side in the shoulder holster. It was almost free when he felt the numbing punch of a round in his right shoulder, followed by pain streaking like lightning down his arm and into his hand. The impact was enough to knock him against the car behind him. Losing his balance, he fell to the ground on his back, his gun skittering out of his reach under the Crown Vic.

Twisting his head towards the front end of his car, he could see feet moving quickly around the front of the Nissan towards the Crown Vic. He reached for the Colt with his left hand, felt the edge of the knurled grip with his fingertips, and stretching as far as he could, managed to finally grasp the handle.

Once he had the Colt in his hand, he rolled onto his back and looked up to see Joey's bulk looming above him and blocking out the sky. The end of the suppressor facing him looked like a very large and expanding black hole. He felt himself being pulled towards it.

Moving in what felt like slow motion, he lifted the Colt with his left hand. Despite the pain in his right shoulder, he disengaged the gun's thumb safety. The hole in front of the suppressor seemed even larger, taking up most of his field of vision. Aiming for what he hoped was Joey's center mass, he pulled the Colt's trigger, fired, fired again, and then again, and again, unable to stop. Only by firing over and over could he hope to avoid dying. Flecks of blacktop sprayed against his face as a stray round from Joey's gun ricocheted off the ground.

The gun and suppressor fell to the blacktop next to him. Joey collapsed against the hood of the Crown Vic before rolling off, landing on the ground in front of the car.

Boone lay there, closing his eyes against the bright sunlight, trying to slow his breathing, trying not to throw up, and trying not to scream with the pain now spreading into his chest. He could hear only a high-pitched, constant whistling sound that blocked out everything else, even the sirens converging on the parking lot.

TWENTY

HE WOKE UP TO see Marianne sitting in a chair on the left side of his bed. It took some time for him to realize he was in a hospital. His right arm was immobilized, his left hand hurt like hell, and his mouth felt coated like the inside of a paint can.

He tried speaking, finally saying only, "Where am I?"

"Welcome back," she said. "The doctor told me you might wake up today. You're at Albany Med. You want some ice chips?"

He nodded.

"I'll let them know you're awake and get some ice. Don't go anywhere. Just lie there."

As if! he thought.

In what seemed to him days later, she was back with a plastic cup full of ice chips.

"Here you go," she said, placing a small one on his lips.

As he got used to taking them, she gave him larger pieces until the cup was empty.

"More?"

He moved his head from side to side, exhausted with even that much effort.

Marianne returned to her seat. After a moment, she said in a shaky voice, "I never realized how committed you were to me when I was so bad off in the hospital until now. I can't tell you how grateful I am for the chance to do the same for you."

He gave no sign that he heard her.

Hours later, he once again opened his eyes. Marianne was still seated in the chair next to his bed.

This time, speaking seemed easier. "What is today?"

"Sunday," she replied. "You've been here two days since you were shot. Want some more ice chips?"

Moving his head from side to side, he said, "Water." Then, "Please."

"I'll be right back." She left the room.

Returning with a cup full of water and a flexible plastic straw, she was accompanied by a young man in a long white coat, a stethoscope jammed into one of the coat's deep pockets. Boone took him for a doctor, even though he looked like a seventeen-year-old.

The doctor slowly raised the head of the bed half-way up. Marianne brought the cup and straw up to his lips, and Boone slowly sipped the best water he had ever tasted in his life.

"Good afternoon, Mr. Boone. I'm Doctor Jansen. How are we feeling today?"

"I've felt better," he said, thinking his voice sounded different, muffled.

"You're a very lucky man," the doctor said.

Thinking, *If I were lucky, I wouldn't be here,* Boone simply nodded.

"Aside from some lumps and bumps, you have some damage to your upper right arm and shoulder, which we've repaired to the extent possible, and a broken little finger on your left hand."

"We removed the bullet arthroscopically, cleaned up the joint debris and stabilized the joint and fracture points. Fortunately, the bullet missed the subclavian artery and the brachial plexus."

Going for humor, Boone said, "What's the bad news? You said I was lucky."

The doctor smiled. "You have some extensive physical therapy after you leave here, as well as additional surgeries to remove the plate and screws we had to install to stabilize the humerus. We expect you'll have nerve damage that will affect your use of your right arm and hand until the nerves regenerate. That will take time."

"How much time?"

"As much as they need. Nerves usually regenerate, if they're going to, at the rate of about an inch a month. It may take up to a year in total."

"What's the prognosis?" he asked.

"Optimistically, you'll recover most of your range of motion and physical capability of your right arm. Worst case? Maybe you'll only get forty to sixty percent of the way there, but it's better, much better than what could have happened. The shoulder joint is probably the most complex joint in the body. Had the bullet struck half an inch higher, we'd be having a very different conversation."

"I'll leave you for the time being. Other visitors are waiting to see you."

Boone said, "Thanks," as the doctor left the room.

Detective George Tucker almost knocked Jansen over in his haste entering the room.

"Carl! It's so good to see you awake. How you doin'?"

Boone shrugged.

"Just wanted to let you know we have an ID for the guy who shot you."

"Oh?"

"Joseph McMurray. He's well known to us. Acts as an enforcer for hire. The only ID on him was a driver's license in his back pocket. We went through his car, and aside from insurance papers and registration, there was nothing. Any idea why he had such a hard-on for you?"

Boone sighed. "I think he worked for Abe Creekson, but I can't prove it."

"What makes you think it was Creekson?"

"I'm working a piece of that file for someone else. The dealer that sold the Creekson boy the GHB in his system was murdered and dumped behind the New Karner Road post office. Abe Creekson has a separate PO Box there. McMurray came to my office twice to threaten me if I didn't lay off the file, and once, when I was surveilling Creekson's office, I saw McMurray going in there."

"We'll keep digging," Tucker said.

"Try the car," Boone said.

"We already did."

"No. I mean check with Nissan. Find out which dealer first sold it and to who. Work it backwards like that. Maybe Creekson or his company bought it."

Tucker pulled a notepad out of his shirt pocket and wrote something down. "Good idea, Carl. I'll get right on that."

"Any other news? Like on Hirschhorn?"

The corners of Tucker's lips turned down in an exaggerated frown. "Nope. Nothing yet anyway."

"Thanks for coming in, George."

"No problem, Carl. You just concentrate on getting better, okay."

"Do my best."

Clive Townsend was the next person to come in the room.

"You know," he snarled, "if you were any better, you'd never let that guy get so close to you."

"Love you too, Clive."

"Until I saw the news about the shooting, I was wondering what happened to you when I didn't hear from you Friday."

"I got sidetracked."

"Did you ever get a chance to meet with that shrink I sent you to?"

A blank expression flitted across Boone's face before he said, "Holy shit!"

"What shit?" Clive said.

"I just remembered. I was supposed to meet with her Saturday night."

"Kinda late for an interview, isn't it?"

Marianne interjected, "That wouldn't be Ms. Pussmaid, would it?"

Boone looked at her, wincing with the effort it took to turn his head. "Yeah. How do you know?"

"You're okay there," Marianne said. "She left voice mail at the office saying she just heard about you on the news, and to let her know when you could have visitors. She said she was very sorry to hear about it."

"You haven't answered my question," Clive said. "Why talk to her so late on a Saturday?"

"I already spoke with her at her office. Saturday evening was, . . . well, . . . a dinner out. Social, you know?"

"I'll be dipped!" Clive said. "And here I thought you were a confirmed isolationist."

"It's just dinner," Boone said.

"Okay. When you feel up to it, call me on Creekson."

"Will do," Boone said as he closed his eyes.

The last thing he remembered was hearing Marianne whispering to Clive, something about 'needs to rest.'

* * *

Boone was near the end of his post-op rehab at Albany Medical when Detective Tucker stopped by.

"How you doing, Carl?"

Sweating profusely as he tried squeezing a stiff rubber ball with his right hand, Boone said,

"What do you want, George? You gonna take me for another ride?"

Tucker sat down in a nearby chair. "No. Just wanted to tell you there's no more problems for you on that Hirschhorn murder case and the thirty-eight. It's all gone away."

Boone gave up on the ball and walked over to a lateral tension station. He pulled the gym towel on his shoulders, rolled it up, and tucked it under his right armpit. He then gripped the handle attached to a weighted cable and began his first set of six reps, drawing the handle across his midsection as well as his hand would allow.

"How is that file gone away?"

"Albany PD got a nine-one-one call last night from the Hirschhorn widow. It seems Grimme decided to tune her up. While they were playing tag in the house, she grabbed her late husband's old thirty-eight police special and took Grimme out with it. Ballistics determined it was the same gun used to kill her husband. So that file's closed."

"Oh." Boone stopped his exercising for the moment. "How bad was she hurt?"

Tucker shook his head. "A real waste, that," he said. "She's going to need a lot of work to look even close to normal. Don't know if she'll get it where she's going."

"Where's that?"

"She claims Grimme killed her husband, even though last night, she said she was the only one who knew where her old man's gun was. We'll see how her questioning goes, but she'll be charged with accessory to murder of her husband, if not murder second. One of those charges is going to stick for sure. She's in the hospital for now."

"Where? Saint Pete's? Ellis?"

"Nope. Here. You want to pay her a visit?"

"No." Boone resumed his exercise. "All I want to do is get outta here this afternoon, and eventually back to work."

He smiled and began counting out his reps.

"Okay, Carl. See you around," Tucker said. "I got things to take care of."

"Me too," Boone replied. "This is my last set of exercises here."

"You get out today you said?"

"Yep. I get discharged this afternoon and start my outpatient physical therapy next week."

"You need any help with anything?"

"No, thanks. I'm all set there."

"Good. See ya."

He left Boone counting, "... two, three, four, ..."

TWENTY-ONE

"How do you feel?"

"With my hands," Boone replied, thinking his voice sounded to him like it was coming through a scratchy speaker.

"But not your right hand," she said.

"Details," he said.

Marianne was taking him home in his Crown Vic. Aside from a baked-on bloodstain on the front of the hood, the car came out of the parking lot gunplay with no apparent damage.

Sitting in his own car with someone else driving was an unfamiliar experience for him. But with his right arm in a sling, he had little choice. He asked the physical therapist when he would be done with the sling. The reply was, "You'll know. Trust me." He had no choice but to do so.

"Deborah still behind us?"

Rolling her eyes, Marianne answered, "Again, yes. Give it a rest, will you? You're like a little kid saying, 'Are we there yet' over and over."

"Sorry."

Deborah was Marianne's ride home, once the two of them fixed dinner for Boone and themselves and got him settled for his first night back in his own apartment.

"Look," he said as Marianne neared his apartment, "I think I can drive myself to the office, okay?"

"No," she replied. "I went over your discharge instructions with the nursing supervisor, and it says, 'No driving.' That means none, or not at all, for at least the first two weeks, and then only if feeling has returned to your right hand."

As she signaled to make the turn into the apartment complex parking lot, she added, "I will be picking you up every morning at seven-thirty. You think you can be ready to go by then?"

"I suppose." He looked out the passenger window, thinking about the week to come. He did not look forward to part time work at the office, and physical therapy three afternoons a week for at least four weeks.

"Anything interesting at the office while I was out?" he asked.

"Again, no. Routine mail, our billings are mostly current. It's fine."

"Any new clients?"

"Yes and no. I have several people looking for an initial appointment. And two previous clients have new concerns for you to look into. That news article about the shooting was great publicity for us. I mean, not that I think your getting shot, . . ."

"I know what you mean, and it's okay. Anything interesting?"

"Mostly routine stuff. A wife who thinks her husband is cheating, an employer worried about his secretary embezzling small amounts from the company. And Clive says he can wait to hear from you on Creekson whenever you're ready."

"Creekson," Boone muttered. "I know he's involved up to his eyeballs in his son's death, but I can't prove it. At least not convincingly."

She turned off the ignition. "Here we are. Can you make it upstairs on your own?"

"My legs aren't in a sling," he said.

"Okay then. You go ahead, I'll bring your bag up."

He waited to open his door until Deborah had parked her BMW on his side and got out of her car. Then, opening his door, he realized how much he depended on his right arm in just getting in and out of a car. Especially out of his beast. *This will not be fun!*

He reached his front door before the two women, but had to stand there, since Marianne had his keys. She was stopping at his mailbox on the first floor to add his mail to his bag.

She unlocked the door and opened it, stepping aside to let him go first. As soon as he stepped into his apartment, he wanted to tell them to drop whatever they were carrying and leave.

His unfinished breakfast from a week ago still sat on his breakfast table, along with a collection of flies. The air had a musty smell, almost as bad as his gym locker. He couldn't remember if he'd made up the bed before leaving for work.

Turning around, he said, "I need the bathroom. Be right back." He went to his bathroom as quickly as possible, shutting the door behind him. Once inside, he lifted the lid on the toilet and breathed a sigh of relief. He sometimes would forget to flush after taking a leak, but thankfully not last Friday.

He rinsed his hands and face as best he could, and after drying off, went back to the living room, mortified to see Deborah at the kitchen sink rinsing dishes and putting them in the dishwasher, cleaning out the coffeepot and straightening things up. Meanwhile, Marianne was wiping down all the surfaces with a cleaning spray and dishcloth.

What is it about women that makes them kick into high gear when they have a slightly inconvenienced man to fuss over? he wondered.

"Ladies!" he said in a loud voice. "I'm not comatose. I can take care of myself, okay?"

Turning around as she dried her hands, Deborah said, "We know that, Carl. We just want to get things neatened up, so you don't have a lot of unnecessary work to start off. Once we leave after dinner, you are on your own."

"Okay," he said. "I'll just sit down here and look at my mail."

Sitting down on his couch, he opened the top of his bag and pulled out a stack of envelopes and circulars. Underneath everything was a copy of the July/August issue of Private Investigator Magazine headlining the '2021 Annual Surveillance Issue.' It was in rough shape, being crammed into a small box along with more mail than the box could hold.

As he sorted the mail into junk, personal mail, and invoices, he listened to the two women talking in low tones, able to catch only the occasional 'him' and 'Carl' as they spoke. His hearing still hadn't fully recovered to his pre-shooting status, which was less than optimal to begin with. He had what doctors called 'shooter's ear' even before he had to fire his Colt four times next to his unprotected ears.

In confined spaces, like his car, he could hear someone speaking reasonably well, but not so well in open spaces. He became aware of Deborah moving in front of the coffee table. Looking up, he could see she was speaking to him. He cupped one hand behind his ear, and she spoke louder.

"Carl?"

"Yeah?"

"We're thinking takeout for tonight. It'll be easier. Any preferences?"

"Otis and Oliver's," he said. "And I'd like their ribs, please."

"Got it," she said. "I'll check with Marianne and go from there."

He nodded before returning to his mail sorting, looking up only as Deborah bustled past with her car keys in hand.

Marianne came into the room, sat down next to him, and placed one hand on his knee, a gesture he found comforting. He turned his head to look at her.

"Thanks," he said.

"For what?"

"Everything, you know."

She shook her head, her eyes glittering like emeralds. "When they called me to tell me, . . . you'd been, . . . I'm sorry." Sniffing, she bowed her head and wiped her eyes before continuing. "I'm just glad you're back, and happy to help even a little bit."

She was going to say more when she heard the sound of an incoming call on her cell. Standing up, she answered.

"Hello?"

"Be right there."

She hung up. Turning to face him, she said, "Deborah's back. Needs help with bringing up the food. Okay?"

He nodded, dropped the rest of his mail in a pile on the coffee table, and leaned back into the couch.

TWENTY-TWO

BOONE WAS TWO WEEKS into his outpatient physical therapy and making small gains daily. He could more easily grip the stress ball with his right hand, even if squeezing it was another matter. He knew it would be a while before he'd be able to take his Colt to the range. Like most semi-automatics, it had a grip safety. A weak grip was certain to result in stovepipe malfunctions, where the brass failed to eject after firing, or worse, the entire round would be trapped in a vertical position between the slide and the firing chamber. *Maybe it's time to consider a more up-to-date carry piece,* he thought.

Marianne was his daily chauffer to and from the office, but he insisted on walking to his PT location, which was only four blocks down South Pearl.

Deborah was coming by his apartment twice a week, either to bring something from home, or to shop and cook something in his kitchen. At first, he objected, worried this was too inconvenient for her. But as he came to enjoy her company, he found it depressing to be alone in his apartment on the nights she wasn't there.

One Wednesday morning near the end of the month, he was looking through his mail while Marianne was at work on her side of the office, when she yelled, "Boss! Look at the Times-Union front page online!"

He dropped what he was working on, bringing up the Albany Times-Union website to see the article that so excited Marianne.

Area Developer killed in murder-suicide

Albany police confirmed the murder-suicide Tuesday of Albany developer Abraham Creekson and his wife, Marilyn Creekson, after finding their bodies at their home on Rafts Way. Police were notified by a housekeeper who discovered the bodies. Initial findings suggest the couple had been dead since the previous Saturday.

Preliminary investigation suggests that Mrs. Creekson killed her husband with a handgun registered to Mr. Creekson before committing suicide by hanging herself.

No motive has been disclosed by the police, which are still investigating. This is a developing story.

Written by
Chris Lyons

Chris Lyons is a political and investigative reporter for the Capitol bureau and contributor to Capitol Confidential.

His first thought was that Marilyn Creekson had somehow discovered her husband's role in the death of her son and could no longer live with it, or herself. But it also meant that he, and Clive Townsend, would never know the truth as far as Geraldine Bronson's role in whatever happened that evening in the Creekson home.

He called Clive, and the two spoke. After some desultory conversation, Clive suggested Boone close his file, and Boone regretfully agreed with him. He hated closing a file without a definitive resolution.

* * *

Two days later, he had all the answers. In Friday morning's mail, he received a letter-sized manila envelope addressed to him and marked 'Personal and Confidential.' There was no return address on the piece, which felt like it contained a magazine or a small stack of paper.

Opening the envelope, he pulled out a handwritten note, and a magazine folded open to an inside page. At the top of the page was a photograph titled 'Boy in a Dream,' featuring a recumbent young man with the face cropped out of the image. Aside from a heavy gold link bracelet on the right-hand wrist, the figure was nude, with his tumescent penis on display.

Underneath the photograph was an article listing the person submitting the photograph as one 'Abe C.'

Scanning the article, Boone read, "Our life-member Abe C. submitted this month's photograph. We are proud to feature it in our bulletin. Abe tells us this young man has been under his care since childhood and has fully embraced the healthy and lasting relationship that can only develop between a boy and an older man." He didn't bother with the rest of it.

Flipping the magazine closed, he saw it was the Man-Boy Love Bulletin from several months back. The address label was Abe C. with a post office box address in Albany, which Boone suspected would be the New Karner Road post office. The cover mentioned other articles within, which ran the gamut from 'Boy 'Victim' Speaks Out' to 'Michael Jackson's Dangerous Liaisons.' Boone laid it to one side and picked up the note.

> *Mr. Boone—I am sending this to you because I believe you will not conceal it to shield my husband as powerful interests might try. Please, I beg of you, do not disappoint me.*
>
> *I found this in his desk, hidden away under business files. At first, I could not understand why my husband would have such material. When I came upon the photograph of my son, I thought I would die. I purchased that bracelet for him for his sixteenth birthday. I would recognize him anywhere, even with his face hidden.*

I confronted my husband with this trash, and he said that he had been, as he put it, 'loving' David since my son could walk. He claimed David was a receptive and willing partner until recently. In the last few years, he sensed David was moving away from him. He did not think he could bear it. If he could not have David as his lover, no one else would.

He said he did not think the young lady would die from the dosed glass of water he gave her when she arrived, and that her death was 'unfortunate.' I do not believe him. My husband has never regretted a single thing in his entire life.

I have thrown away my own life living with a monster. There is but only one outcome to make this right.

M.

Boone laid the note to one side, tormented by the utter destruction of three promising lives to sate one man's sense of personal indulgence. Picking up the phone, he called Clive. After speaking with him, he next called Elaine Russell.

EPILOGUE

AFTER FOUR WEEKS OF Deborah's providing dinners two or three times a week, she announced that after her next visit, Boone would be on his own for evening meals. To celebrate, she planned to bring dinner from Delmonico's Italian Steakhouse.

"But don't think this lets you off the hook from taking me out to dinner!" she said.

That evening, she let herself in with the entrees, using the key he had given her.

"I'll be right back with the rest," she said. "Why don't you open a bottle of wine?"

Knowing he would no longer have her company to look forward to in the evenings, he was feeling sorry for himself.

When she returned, she had a small bag of side dishes from the restaurant and a small suitcase.

"What's the suitcase for?" he asked.

"Oh, you know. Pajamas, and personal items."

Feeling the ground shifting under him, he was not certain what to say. "Uh, . . . I mean, . . . well, . . . I don't have a guest room set up."

"Carl," she said. "I'm forty-eight years old. I know how this works."

AUTHOR'S NOTE

BOONE is the first book in a series involving Carl Boone and Marianne Bell after the events in *Unaccountable*. Always wanting to try my hand at a detective story, I hope this effort does not disappoint.

The two story arcs deal with pornography and pedophilia.

Studies suggest that over 85% of men view pornography weekly, contrasted with only 29% of women. Adult women must not be looking at very much pornography, if 57% of all fourteen- to eighteen-year-old- females are checking it out in the fair sex. Overall, pornography is featured on only 4% of websites, but accounts for 20% of all web searches.

There are any number of websites and publications dealing with the grooming of young boys by older men for homosexual relationship, including *boylinks.org, NAMBLA.org, freerangekids.com,* and Modern Boy Lover Magazine. Anyone interested in further research will have no difficulty finding them.

As for the rapidly proliferating use of drugs in conjunction with sex, especially among younger people with so-called club drugs like MDMA or GHB, the web is replete with studies by Kaiser Permanente, NIH and the CDC regarding the usage and effects (both temporary and long-term). By the time they reach the age of eighteen, nearly 47% of young people have experimented with illicit drugs, and twelve million eighteen to twenty-five year olds have used drugs in the previous month.

I thank my advance readers for their many suggestions and advice. But most of all, I am grateful for the never-ending love and support of my wife, Donna.

Frederic W. Burr
September 2021

www.ingramcontent.com/pod-product-compliance
Ingram Content Group UK Ltd.
Pitfield, Milton Keynes, MK11 3LW, UK
UKHW022210230426
12048UKWH00016BA/750